# THE GOLDEN GIRL

Adrian Belmont had transformed Rosamund from a half-hearted amateur to an Olympics class runner—and of course as a result she had fallen in love with him. But he never seemed to see her as a woman—and why should he, since he was going to marry the sophisticated French girl Madeleine Delaney?

*Books you will enjoy*
*by* ELIZABETH ASHTON

**THE QUESTING HEART**

Clare wanted to write a romantic novel—but how could she, when she had no experience whatsoever of love and romance, so how could she do it convincingly? Then she met Chris Raines, who was certainly romantic and a man of the world—but wasn't she rather inexperienced for a man like him? And wouldn't any experience she shared with him be hurtful rather than useful?

**BREEZE FROM THE BOSPHORUS**

Venice had been persuaded by her friend Selma to go with her to Turkey, where a marriage was to be arranged for Selma with either Kemal or Ahmet Osman. It was Kemal who was eventually chosen—which was a pity, as by that time Venice had fallen in love with him herself!

**GREEN HARVEST**

Julian Everard had always been the only man in the world for Toni—but although admitting her attraction, he had always refused to take her seriously. She made a new life for herself, but even so, she could never manage to put him out of her heart. Would she ever be able to overcome this hopeless love?

**AEGEAN QUEST**

The lordly Nikolaos Palaeologus was descended from the Byzantine emperors, and he certainly didn't think a nobody like Prunella Paterson— who was actually on the *stage*!—was a fit person to marry his young brother Leo. Prunella's more spirited sister Priscilla took it upon herself to challenge him—with results that she had not bargained for . . .

# THE
# GOLDEN GIRL

BY
ELIZABETH ASHTON

**MILLS & BOON LIMITED**
17–19 FOLEY STREET
LONDON W1A 1DR

*First published 1978*
*Australian copyright 1978*
*Philippine copyright 1978*
*This edition 1978*

© Elizabeth Ashton 1978

ISBN 0 263 72636 3

*Set in Linotype Times 10 on 11½ pt.*

*Made and printed in Great Britain by*
*Richard Clay (The Chaucer Press), Ltd., Bungay, Suffolk*

# CHAPTER ONE

THE girl crouched on top of the high wall surveyed the parkland spread below her, a green expanse dotted with stands of trees, thrusting bare branches towards the pale blue sky, and the occasional single majestic oak, the product of decades of slow growth. The ground was strewn with daffodils, an early bloom a spot of colour here and there a promise of the sheet of gold they would later display.

It was a mild afternoon in early spring, and the typically English scene was beautiful in its pastoral serenity, but the girl eyed it with a frown between her level dark brows; she had not attained her precarious perch to admire the view.

The house which the park enclosed was veiled by a phalanx of beech trees, showing a glimpse of red brick between their trunks. Belmont House, home of Adrian Belmont, rich man, ex-athlete, well-known sports promoter and running coach, who for a hobby, and to her mind out of pure cussedness, inaugurated training courses for budding athletes on his own estate, from which women were rigorously excluded. She was hating him badly, and with just cause; she had a perfectly legitimate reason for coming to see Tony Bridges, and he had no right to deny her admission. The place was not a prison and her request that a message be delivered to him was quite reasonable; he would have come at once if he had known she was there. That, she was told, was against the rules, moreover she had been insulted.

Rosamund Prescott was not a girl who accepted defeat easily. By fair means or foul she was determined to accomplish her mission.

The formidable brick wall that encircled the park with spikes on top of it was almost impossible to scale, but luck favoured her. At one point, some quarter of a mile from the main gate, a small van had been parked against it, and above it several of the spikes had been broken off, and not yet been repaired. In a matter of seconds Rosamund had swarmed up on to the roof of the van and thence on to the top of the wall. Lithe and agile as she was, the feat had been easy, and now she could see that the drop on the other side was not so great as that to the road, with soft turf to alight upon. Once she was among the trees in the park she could hide until she had located Tony.

Tony Bridges was her special boy-friend and today was her birthday. Before he went away, Tony himself had declared that it was a date he could not break and she must join him in Surrey, where they would celebrate it together whatever other commitments he had, but when she had written to remind him of his promise, he had replied that it was not possible. Days off were only permitted for emergencies, and Mr Belmont was prejudiced against girl-friends, declaring that their influence was detrimental to young athletes. Tony would see her as soon as the course was over, which would not be long now, but would she please keep away from Belmont House.

Rosamund was furious, and her anger was directed nearly as much against the unreasonable Mr Belmont as at Tony's refusal to see her. She was sure that he could have engineered a meeting somehow, but he feared being sent away in disgrace more than he wanted to see her. But surely Mr Belmont could not be quite so tyrannical as to do that? She took a bus from London to the village that served the estate, determined to demand to see Tony, and if the owner denied her, to tell him what she thought of his ridiculous regulations.

She was unable to gain access to either of them.

The tall iron gates that guarded the approach to the house were padlocked and the lodge-keeper who came out in response to her call told her firmly that he could not admit her. Strangers, especially female ones, were forbidden entrance to Belmont House by the master's orders. Surely Mr Bridges had told her so?

'But I'm not exactly a stranger,' Rosamund had protested. 'Can't you give him a message? Tell him I'm waiting to see him?'

The man shrugged his shoulders and grinned insolently.

'That would be as much as my place is worth, miss. We've plenty of dames trying to contact our young athletes; such fine young fellows draw 'em like wasps to jam, but master's very strict, has to be for their protection.'

Swallowing her pride, and disliking him intensely, Rosamund had pleaded with him. She had come a long way, she was Tony Bridges' fiancée, which was stretching a point, there was as yet no engagement between them, and surely that gave her a right of entry? Or at least to have a word with him if he could be advised of her presence?

The man remained adamant.

'They all have women claiming to be fiancées,' he had told her. 'Most of 'em aren't anything of the sort, just tarts.'

Rosamund's fury increased, but there was nothing to

be gained by bandying words with this oaf who had insulted her. She left the gate, vowing she would find some way in and make her complaint to Tony. He would be as angry as she was at her reception, and if Adrian Belmont was available, she would tell him what she thought of his objectionable gate-keeper. But the place seemed to be impregnable, with no opening in the high brick wall except the guarded gate.

So that was how she came to be perched on the top of that same wall considering her next move.

Rosamund's father, Paul Prescott, had always been interested in athletics and when at school his daughter had shown running potential, he had encouraged and trained her. The girl herself had found pleasure and exhilaration in the sport, which was one thing she could do well, not being academically or artistically gifted. In her teens she had won the English Schools Championship as a sprinter. When she left school she joined an athletic club, but her enthusiasm waned, to the disappointment of her father and the club coaches. Running took up too much time, and winter training was a bore when there were so many other interesting things to do. She ran occasionally but did not distinguish herself, and she liked the club for its social amenities. It was there she had met Tony Bridges. He was a keen sportsman, specialising in the mile, but not so much so that he excluded other activities, like dancing which they both enjoyed. He did not encourage rivalry from her, saying one athlete in a family was enough, which indicated that he was contemplating marrying her, though he was a little vague about his intentions. Rosamund was confident that they would eventually marry, she believed she was in love with him, but she was only twenty and eager to see more of life before she settled down.

It was at an indoor sports meeting in February that Tony had encountered Adrian Belmont. They had both been competing, neither very brilliantly. Tony had pointed Adrian out to her where he was sitting among a group of officials. She had glimpsed a fine Roman head with an aquiline nose and jet black hair, and had exclaimed in surprise:

'Why, he's quite young!'

'I suppose he must be.' Tony was not interested in Adrian's age. 'All the more remarkable that he's a V.I.P. in British athletics. He has his own track at his place in Surrey and occasionally he runs a course for promising runners. What wouldn't I give to attract his notice!'

Rosamund came in last in her event, and did not mind; Tony failed to make a qualifying time and was dejected, but his depression was changed to elation by the end of the evening, when he came to join Rosamund after they had changed, bubbling with excitement.

'Guess what, he's spoken to me! Says I've got style and stamina and if I can increase my speed I'm a potential champion. He's asked me to go to Belmont for a month's intensive training at Easter. I hope my firm will let me take my holiday then and grant me the extra time, but with the bank holidays ...'

Rosamund cut in anxiously: 'Tony, you can't be away at Easter. We're invited to Sara's wedding, and we were going to have a week away together.'

'Darling, I'm sorry about all that, but don't you see, this is a unique opportunity.'

She had to agree in the end; she could not stand in the way of Tony's chances, though she thought privately that Adrian Belmont's prestige was overrated and his boasted track a piece of self-advertisement.

'I'll be able to come and see you?'

'I'm afraid not. It's an intensive course and everyone knows Mr Belmont allows no distractions. He's got a thing about girls, says they're lethal to an athlete's chances.'

'He must be nuts,' Rosamund had cried indignantly. 'Haven't I always supported and encouraged you?'

'You have, darling. He must have been crossed in love at some time, that does affect some men's morale, though I'm sure it would never upset me. I'll miss you terribly, but it's only for a month.'

'Which includes my birthday. We made that a special date.'

'And still will,' Tony assured her. 'We'll keep that wherever I am, it's a special occasion.'

Now he declared it was impossible.

Rosamund unslung her shoulder bag and dropped it over the wall, on to a pile of dead leaves. Then she slipped over herself, taking a firm grip of two of the spikes as she lowered herself her full length to lessen the distance. She landed lightly on the soft turf, collapsing in a relaxed heap. Jumping to her feet, she glanced ruefully at the green marks on her skirt and shoes and wished she had worn jeans, but she had not anticipated having to overcome such an obstacle and her denim skirt and sweater had been chosen for her meeting with Tony, who preferred feminine fashions.

Picking up her bag, she looked about her seeking cover among the trees, and then she froze, for coming towards her was a man, accompanied by two large red setters. Had he been alone, she would have run trusting to be able to outdistance him, but dogs were another matter, they would catch her before she had gone a few yards. All she could do was to stand still and brazen it out.

The man came nearer and with a catch of her breath she recognised him. She had attained one of her objectives, for he was Adrian Belmont himself. Having once seen those distinctive features there was no mistaking him. She drew herself up, her eyes gleaming—now she could tell him what she thought of his tyrannical ways, and his odious gate-keeper!

He paused a few yards away from her, commanding his dogs to sit. He carried a stout walking stick and from his expression he would not scruple to use it upon her if she gave him provocation. But Rosamund was not intimidated, and held her bright head high. He was wearing a black track suit piped with white, and she noticed with surprise that his eyes under the slightly tilted dark brows were piercingly blue, contrasting with his tanned face and ebony hair. As he regarded her slim boyish figure, her elfin face with the determined chin outthrust, her red-gold hair a nimbus in the sunlight, his face cleared and his lips twitched, and when he spoke his tone was more of wonderment than of anger.

'How the devil did you get here?'

'Over the wall,' she informed him frostily.

'Did you, by Jove?' His eyes went to the imposing height of bricks behind her. 'Quite a feat, but then nothing can deter a determined woman. You're trespassing, my dear, this is private property.'

'I'm well aware of that,' she returned. 'But I wouldn't have been driven to such lengths if your man on the gate had been civil. I only wanted a few words with my boyfriend Tony Bridges, but he refused to admit me.'

'And rightly so. I don't want any amorous young

females invading my privacy and distracting my athletes.'

'You don't understand. I'm Tony Bridges' girl-friend and I've his career just as much at heart as you have. I wouldn't distract him, but we had a date—it's my birthday, and he promised to keep it. I don't see why I can't see him for an hour or so since I've come all this way.'

'I'm sorry, but if I break a rule for one, it would have to be for all, and I will not have females here disturbing the boys' concentration. I pick them with care and they know what's involved, including a denial of feminine society. I regret your wasted journey, but surely Tony told you visitors were forbidden?'

Adrian had a deep pleasant voice and he was reasoning with her calmly, and Tony had told her not to come, so she was in the wrong. But his restraint only irritated her the more. She would have been better pleased if he had abused her, thus giving her cause for resentment. Moreover, there was something disturbing about this man's personality that affected her against her will. She was not normally susceptible to masculine allure, but she was subtly aware of this man's magnetism, and his attractiveness increased rather than decreased her resentment against him. She would not allow him to deflect her from her purpose almost within sight of her objective. Through the trees she glimpsed several distant figures in running shorts, one of which might well be Tony. She would have risked a dash towards them if it had not been for the dogs, and though they were sitting placidly one on each side of their master, their watchful eyes followed her every movement.

'What is this place?' she demanded contemptuously, ignoring his question. 'A monastery? It couldn't possibly harm Tony to see me for a few moments. Your rules are ridiculous, Mr Belmont.'

His well-shaped mouth set in a hard line.

'Perhaps, but they *are* my rules. Allow me to escort you to the gate.'

Her eyes flashed defiantly. 'You may not! I intend to stay here.' She glanced towards the distant figures. 'If I shout he'll hear me.'

'He isn't there,' he told her. His glance slid appreciatively over her taut figure and rested upon the copper-gold of her hair. 'He's in the gym. What a little firebrand you are, but your obduracy will avail you nothing.' His hand went to a whistle he wore on a cord about his neck. 'If you won't go quietly, I'll have to have you put out.'

Rosamund met his cold blue gaze without flinching, her own eyes gleaming. She had beautiful eyes of amber colour surrounded by long dark lashes, as he had already noticed.

'Go on, Mr Belmont, summon your thugs,' she taunted him. 'It's what I'd expect from a tyrant like you, but a man in your position ought to be more civilised.'

'It's your position that is questionable, not mine,' he returned coldly. 'Mine is assured.' His face softened and he added coaxingly, 'Come, girl, you know you're trespassing, don't force me to do something so distasteful.'

'Distasteful?' she echoed disdainfully. 'Don't be a hypocrite, you'd enjoy seeing me thrown out, wouldn't you? You're a despot, Mr Belmont, every line of your bearing betrays your arrogance. You like bullying your boys ... and me!'

But he was not listening.

'You seem to know my name,' he remarked wonderingly. 'But I've never seen you before, have I?'

'Of course you must be Mr Belmont of Belmont House, you couldn't be anyone else,' she flashed back. 'But I saw you at the sports meeting where you became interested in Tony.'

'Ah yes, and you ran yourself, I recall, in the four hundred metres.'

'I'm surprised you noticed me.'

He smiled quizzically. 'Your hair is unusual. It's a beautiful colour.'

'I'm not to be cajoled by flattery,' she said stiffly. 'And I didn't distinguish myself. I came in last, but I'm not a serious athlete like Tony.'

'Then you should be,' he told her, assessing her slim, lithe figure. Rosamund was five foot six, and in spite of her slenderness, there was supple strength in her shoulders and long straight legs. 'For a girl you showed good form, a nice long stride, and I can see you have stamina.'

'But I didn't even try to win,' she gasped, taken aback by this analysis.

'That's a feeble confession. Why run at all if you don't want to win? You could have done.'

'It gives me some exercise,' she explained, 'but to win I'd have to train much harder and it's such a drag.' An impish light came into her eyes. 'You consider yourself a sportsman, don't you, Mr Belmont? You've been a runner, I believe. I'll race you to that tree,' she waved towards a distant oak, 'and if I beat you, you'll let me see Tony? That'll give me an inducement to exert myself.'

An intense bitterness distorted his face, drawing grooves between his brows and from nose to mouth.

'Nothing doing, my dear. My racing days are done.'

He indicated his leg with his stick, and it was only then that it occurred to her that he used a stick because he needed its support. Adrian Belmont, once an international champion, was lame. Overcome by contrition, she began to stammer:

'I'm sorry, I'd no idea, nobody told me ...'

'Do you think I'd spend my time training others if I could still compete myself?' he demanded harshly. 'I'm not yet too old.' His gaze went beyond her to the soft blue sky above the wall. 'I'd set my heart on an Olympic gold, but I never won one. This happened,' he again indicated his knee, 'before I could.'

Silence fell between them, the man recalling his lost ambition, the girl wondering what she could say to retrieve her blunder. One of the dogs moved restlessly, rustling some dead leaves, far overhead a lark was singing. Tony had implied that Adrian Belmont had retired, but he had never hinted that it was a forced retirement because of injury. He must know that now, but he had never mentioned it in his letters, and she, seeing Adrian Belmont looking so strong and virile, had never suspected it.

Adrian Belmont brought his gaze back to her face and the compassion he saw there caused him to grimace; he hated pity.

'But I accept your challenge,' he told her. 'I can't run myself, but my dogs can. If you can beat Roland to that tree, you shall see your boy-friend.'

Rosamund looked at the two dogs. They were beautiful, powerful creatures, and though they looked amiable enough, with their tongues lolling, she could see their strong white fangs. She had no guarantee that they would not fly at her throat if their master relaxed his guard; they were probably trained to intercept intruders. She was unused to dogs and a little afraid of them, especially big brutes like these two. She moistened her lips with her tongue and met Adrian Belmont's eyes, surprising in their blue depths a glint of cruelty. Divining her fear, he had devised this ordeal to punish her for daring to defy him.

'I ... I ...' she stammered, her hands going to her throat, 'I don't think I can. To run against dogs—it's gruesome!'

'People frequently run with dogs,' he pointed out, 'and Roland won't hurt you. I'm not proposing to loose them both, they'd get too excited.' He smiled scornfully. 'Chicken?'

Rosamund quivered at the taunt.

'If I win ... I may see Tony?'

'Didn't I say so?'

Rosamund squared her shoulders and slipped off her shoulder bag, threw one anxious glance at the red dogs and without giving herself time to think further, cried: 'Well, here goes!'

She sprang forward like a gazelle and sped over the grass towards the tree. She heard Adrian's word of command and knew she was pursued, but resolutely refrained from glancing back over her shoulder towards the leaping form behind her. The other dog, held back from joining in the chase, whined and howled, adding an eerie accompaniment to the race. Rosamund experienced in those few seconds all the terror of a hunted creature pursued by a predatory foe. In imagination she felt the dog's teeth in her leg. It even crossed her mind that Adrian might be kinky enough to have deliberately loosed his dog to savage her. No one would know that it had not come upon her trespassing, and she would have suffered a cruel retribution before he called it off.

The tree, an ancient oak, was almost within touching distance and she was well ahead of the dog, when she caught her toe in an exposed root and went sprawling.

She felt the dog's breath on her neck and believed her
worst fears were about to be realised, but the beast
merely licked her cheek, and hearing his master's voice
drew away from her. Shakily she sat up and pushed her
hair away from her face. Her hand came away red and
moist and she found she had a gash on her forehead
where it had struck a stone. Hastily she pulled out a
handkerchief from a pocket in her skirt and dabbed at
it; it seemed to be bleeding profusely.

Adrian Belmont reached her, and dropping his stick,
knelt beside her.

'Hell, I never meant this to happen,' she heard him
mutter. Very gently he moved her hand from her face.
'Let me look.' Consternation showed on his face as he
exclaimed, 'It's a nasty cut, and that little rag's no good.'

He produced a large white handkerchief from his own
person and bound it round her head. The two dogs pushed
commiserating noses against them until he sternly bade
them remove themselves. Rosamund wondered how she
could have been afraid of such friendly creatures, but
her panic had been very real.

Adrian Belmont sat back on his heels, regarding her
anxiously.

'Do you think you can walk as far as the house, where
I can get my housekeeper to attend to it?'

'Oh, I think so,' she replied, and sprang nimbly to her
feet. A wave of giddiness swept over her and she put out
a groping hand seeking support. He caught it, having
struggled up and regained his stick. He drew it firmly
within his arm.

'Lean on me, I can hold you up, even if I am lame.'
Again the note of bitterness in his quiet voice.

'The halt leading the blind,' Rosamund murmured a
little hysterically, for she was almost painfully conscious

of his muscular arm beneath her hand, and the bandage
was half over her eyes.

'Just so,' he said shortly.

The other dog, Oliver, had meanwhile retrieved her
bag, and he dropped it at her feet, looking up with a
wagging tail for a word of praise.

'Good boy,' Adrian Belmont said, hooking it up with
his stick. Rosamund reached for it with her free hand.

'What an intelligent animal,' she remarked.

'He's been taught to retrieve.' He was guiding her towards the house. 'I'm as competent with animals as with
men.'

He sounded complacent, but Rosamund was sure it
was no idle boast; he would be competent about whatever
he undertook. She had difficulty in restraining her hand
from trembling at the close contact with him. She supposed it was the shock of her fright and her fall, but her
nerve ends were tingling, she had a shrewd suspicion that
Adrian Belmont was dynamite where women were concerned, and she wondered if there were any in his life;
as far as she knew he was not married. Possibly he sensed
something of her inner disquiet, for he said gently:

'I'm afraid you've had a nasty fall. Believe me, I
wouldn't have had that happen for the world.'

'I shouldn't have fallen in with your crazy idea,' she
told him, glancing up at his profile inches from her head.
The nose was straight, the chin square and determined,
denoting a strong will. He turned his head and looked
down into her eyes with a glint in his.

'Idiotic,' he agreed. 'But the result would have been
the same if you ran against a man, and you chose the oak
as a target. You're as fleet as a deer.'

'I've never run faster in my life,' she declared, looking

away from that disconcerting gaze. 'Now I know what hunted slaves felt like!'

'I'm sorry,' he apologised again, 'but my dogs aren't bloodhounds. They wouldn't hurt you, and it seemed an amusing idea.'

'For you perhaps, but not for me,' she returned tartly, regaining something of her normal spirit. 'Do I see Tony now?'

'You'd better be cleaned up first,' he suggested.

'Oh, definitely—he'll hardly be pleased to know that you allowed your dog to savage me.'

'I did no such thing, and well you know it. You tripped over something and Roland never touched you, nor would he.'

She giggled feebly. 'He did, he licked me and didn't like the taste.' An idea occurred to her. She was still resentful of Adrian's high-handedness and angry with herself for her reaction to his masculinity. Intuitively she knew that he expected to get his own way, especially with women.

'But Tony won't know what really happened,' she said sweetly. 'He'll believe what I tell him.'

He stopped, hooked his stick on his arm and turned her to face him. His grip of her shoulders was not gentle.

'You mean you'll say I set the dog on you?' his voice was dangerously quiet and his eyes had the coldness of ice.

'I might.' She tried to wriggle free, but his hold tightened.

'Do you want to make bad blood between us?' he demanded with cold ferocity. 'You tiresome, interfering little bitch! Have you no thought for his ambitions? I can do something for that boy, he has the potential, but if you alienate him from me you'll lessen his chances.

He'll never get a better coach than I am. What's more, I understand how to deal with him—I make a personal study of every youth I undertake to train, and I only train a few. The individual touch means a great deal to a budding athlete, but you're too ignorant to appreciate that.'

She was helpless in his grip and his eyes seemed to bore into her. How very blue they were, she thought irrelevantly, but so frosty and hard, with the force of a steel probe. Involuntarily she shivered as he went on: 'Like all women you delight in making mischief, you're motivated by your petty feminine vanity and you want to show me your power over Tony is greater than all my influence. Well, go ahead, lie to him if you want to, and if later on he realises what you've done to him, I hope he rends you.'

His antagonism was evident in every note of his vibrant voice. How he despises women, was her underlying thought as, stung by his injustice, she cried angrily:

'You're being very unfair, Mr Belmont. You're a double-dyed misanthrope, or do I mean mysogynist? I've no intention of spoiling Tony's athletic career, I wouldn't do that for anything, but if it wasn't for the fact that I believe you *can* help him, I'd take great pleasure in causing you just as much trouble as I possibly could!'

Afterwards she was to wonder at her temerity. Adrian Belmont was a name in sporting circles, and he was the owner of a fine estate, with Tony's future in his hands, while she was a mere nobody, caught invading his territory; moreover, she must be looking a sight with her clothes dusty and dirty, and a handkerchief—his handkerchief—hanging over one eye. If he had abused her it was no more than she deserved by threatening to lie to Tony to make things awkward for him, and now she had been

rude and unpleasant. She half expected he would have
her thrown out despite the wound in her head. Instead of
which he laughed, crinkling up his eyes in an attractive
manner, and his grip of her shoulders slackened.

'That's honest anyway,' he said, 'and I've a hunch
you're going to cause me quite a bit of trouble, my young
spitfire.' Then, noticing how pale she was, and that her
shoulders sagged in spite of her show of defiance, his
face softened. Linking her arm with his again, he told her
gently:

'You're in no state for fireworks, and the sooner that
gash is bathed the better. We'll call a truce for now.'

'Willingly,' Rosamund agreed, for her head was aching
and she was a little ashamed of her outburst. He was
being kinder than she deserved.

They came through the last barrier of trees and the
house was before them, an impressive red brick Georgian
edifice with tall sash windows. Twin pillars supporting a
portico were on either side of the front door, which was
approached by a short flight of steps; a sweep of gravelled
drive led up to it, which curved down through an avenue
of lime trees to the gateway from which she had been
turned away, but the lodge was not visible from the
house.

'Do your trainees live here with you?' she asked, wondering if Tony would appear.

'Good lord, no. They have their own quarters in the
park, a sports complex with a gymnasium and a swimming pool, also a running track. I prefer to be private in
the house, though I'm not really a misanthrope,' he smiled
mockingly. 'I entertain quite a lot.'

'Even so, it looks an enormous place for a ... home,'
she said, thinking of the Prescotts' small suburban house.

'I don't use it all, except when I accommodate a conference for a sports association.' His mouth twisted wryly. 'Though incapacitated myself I retain an interest in the achievements of others.'

She was surprised he could bear to do so, but she said nothing. The dogs raced ahead of them and up the steps into the house, they followed more sedately, Rosamund stumbling a little as she negotiated them. Adrian Belmont put his arm firmly round her waist to assist her, and her fine-spun hair sprayed his shoulder as they entered the hall. To the woman who came hurrying from the back premises they looked like a pair of lovers, and she stared at them in astonishment.

'This young lady has met with a slight accident, Mrs Grey,' Adrian Belmont told her. 'Will you please bring a bowl of warm water and some sticking plaster?'

They had entered a square spacious hall with a fine staircase of polished wood and doors giving access to the rooms on the ground floor. It contained several fine carved chairs and a circular table, with some ancient trophies hanging on the walls, old firearms, a machete, a curved dagger, and crossed swords over one door. Adrian Belmont took Rosamund through the door on the right-hand side, into what seemed to be a kind of office, for its principal furniture was a large desk. There were two leather-covered armchairs on either side of an electric fire, and he lowered her carefully into one of them. The dogs had entered with them, and at the words, 'Go basket,' they retired into large wicker baskets put in one corner.

Mrs Grey came hurrying back carrying a bowl, towels and a first aid box. She was a plump white-haired woman with a rosy, good-natured face. Deftly she removed the makeshift bandage and bathed the cut, while Adrian Belmont leaned against the desk watching her. Behind him on a shelf were rows of silver cups and trophies, and on the walls framed photographs of various teams. Evidently this room was his private sanctum ornamented with the mementoes from his past achievements.

'I could have gone to the bathroom,' Rosamund murmured, eyeing the stained water.

'Couldn't have got you upstairs in your wilting condition,' he explained. 'This was nearer.' He looked at Mrs Grey. 'Do you think it needs a stitch?'

'Oh no, it's not deep. I'll put a dressing on and a strip of plaster. She's a nice healthy skin and it'll soon heal,' Mrs Grey decided. 'How did it happen?'

'She climbed the park wall ...' Adrian began, and she clicked her teeth.

'What a crazy thing to do! She might have broken her neck.' Over her head Adrian and Rosamund's eyes met. Neither of them wanted to enlighten her as to the real cause of the accident. Mrs Grey's broad face creased into a smile. 'After the lads, I'm thinking.'

'One lad,' Adrian corrected her. 'It seems I've imperilled a promising romance with my strictures. Love, we're told, laughs at locksmiths, and in this case climbs unscaleable walls.' He moved to a cupboard which contained bottles and glasses. 'A tot of brandy, Miss ... I don't know your name!'

'Rosamund Prescott,' she said stiffly, annoyed by his facetiousness. 'And I don't drink spirits.'

'I prescribe it as a medicine, and this is mostly soda.' He held up a glass. 'Drink it up, there's a sensible girl.' He handed it to her and poured a stronger potion for himself. 'It'll help you to revive.'

'Best do as the master says,' Mrs Grey admonished her with a twinkle in her bright eyes.

Rosamund obediently drank, making a wry face over

it, but the spirit did revive her. She noticed that in the house Adrian abandoned his stick. He moved about with agility, but his limp was pronounced.

'And now,' she demanded, 'may I see Tony?'

'I'll have him fetched. Tea for three in the drawing room, Mrs Grey. We'll do this in style.'

Rosamund opened her mouth to protest and shut it again without speaking. She could not deny the master his presence in his own house, but she did not want him there when she saw Tony. He was cunning, he would allow her to see her friend, but only under his supervision, and she did not feel protests would be any use.

'Could I ... is there a bathroom?' she enquired. 'I'm strong enough to reach it now, and I'd like to tidy up.'

Mrs Grey conducted her upstairs and into a well-appointed bathroom where Rosamund did her best to repair the ravages of her misadventure, sponging the worst marks off her skirt, combing her hair and making up her face from the contents of her shoulder bag. The plaster was an unsightly blot on her left temple and she tried to arrange her hair to conceal it as much as possible. A sudden tattoo on the door caused her to jump, and a childish voice demanded:

'Want to see the poor cut-up lady!'

She opened the door and found Mrs Grey remonstrating with a small girl of about four or five, who was objecting loudly to being removed.

'Sorry, miss,' Mrs Grey apologised. 'She's a young imp and she gave me the slip.'

'I saw the bowl,' the child announced with ghoulish relish. 'All bleedy.' She stared at Rosamund. 'Where's the cut?'

'Covered up now,' Rosamund told her, concealing her surprise. A young child was the last thing she had ex-

pected to meet in Adrian Belmont's house. She wondered
if she were his, but she had heard no mention of any
family and the round, rosy face and big brown eyes did
not suggest such stern parentage.

'My granddaughter, Lucie,' Mrs Grey explained, as if
guessing her thought. 'Mr Belmont allows me to have
her here. You see, my daughter got married ...' she
hesitated ... 'again and her husband didn't want a babe
that was none of his. Mr Belmont is a most kind and
considerate employer.'

Lucie, disappointed that no gory wound was visible,
had run away during this disclosure, which was a side-
light upon Adrian Belmont. Rosamund reflected that
good housekeepers were not easily come by, and doubt-
less he had agreed to the child's presence to retain the
services of the very capable-looking Mrs Grey. Rosamund was determined not to attribute generous motives
to him.

'If you're ready, miss, shall we go down?' Mrs Grey
enquired. 'The Master is asking for you.'

'And it would never do to keep him waiting,' Rosamund remarked, with a barbed glance that was wasted
upon the simple woman. 'Has Mr Bridges come?'

'Oh yes, miss, the Master sent for him at once. You'll
find them both in the drawing room.'

Rosamund sped downstairs with a light heart. In spite
of high walls, grumpy gate-keepers, guardian dogs and
Adrian Belmont, she had been successful in her undertaking and was about to see Tony.

# CHAPTER TWO

THE drawing room—lounge was too modern a term for such a stately apartment—was at the back of the house with french windows opening on to a lawn surrounded by herbaceous borders. It still preserved the atmosphere of Regency days when it had been in truth a withdrawing room, where ladies of the period presided over the after-dinner tea table. The pattern of the long floor-length curtains and the upholstery was in cream and red stripes, and the furniture looked like Sheraton. The comfortable chesterfield and two armchairs before the log fire burning in the grate below the marble mantelpiece were of a later date.

Tony and Adrian Belmont were standing by the window as Rosamund came in. The latter had changed into trousers and a blue sweater; Tony was similarly clad and he came towards her eagerly holding out his hands. There was nothing distinguished about Tony Bridges, he was an ordinary clean-limbed, fresh-faced English youth, neither handsome nor plain, with brown hair curling to his shoulders and candid hazel eyes. He was clean-shaven because Rosamund had told him she could not abide beards. He kissed her lightly on her cheek, and she was no more affected by his caress than if he had been a brother.

'Well, darling, so you've been in the wars, climbing ten-foot walls!' He shook his head in mock reproof. 'But I did tell you not to come.' He glanced apologetically at Adrian over his shoulder, who was watching them with a sardonic smile upon his well-shaped lips. 'It might have been worse, you could have broken a limb.'

From which she deduced he surmised, like Mrs Grey, that her injury had been caused by falling off the wall.

'It's my birthday,' she said as if that explained everything, and threw Adrian a challenging look.

'I didn't forget. I've sent you a present, hasn't it come yet?'

'I left before the parcel post arrived.'

'I hadn't anticipated that. Well, since you are here, I'm delighted to see you.'

He still held her hands, and rendered self-conscious by Adrian's presence, Rosamund gently withdrew them. If only he would go away and leave them together, but he seemed to have no intention of doing so. Mrs Grey's entrance with the tea tray created a diversion.

Adrian insisted that she must pour out, a woman's privilege, he declared, admitting that he rarely bothered with tea when he was alone. Before she left, Mrs Grey switched on the lights, which were fixed in wall sconces shaped like candles, and drew the curtains to shut out the fading daylight. There was a crystal chandelier above their heads depending from the ceiling, but that was only used upon formal occasions.

Rosamund manipulated the silver teapot and fine china, praying she would not have a mishap. She was usually deft in her movements but Adrian Belmont made her feel clumsy, for his eyes never seemed to leave her and she suspected he was weighing her up and finding her wanting.

Conversation was stilted at first until they got on to running. Then both men became enthusiastic. Adrian told Tony he had a chance of being selected for the European games if he continued to make progress, and Tony proudly told her his time had been only a second short of the record that morning.

'Never did a mile in such fast time before. But the snag is the record is being broken all the time and the speed increased, especially with these types from Kenya competing.'

'Splendid, Tony,' Rosamund encouraged him. 'I'm sure you'll do better still.'

'So long as you keep your mind on the job,' Adrian warned him, glancing meaningly at Rosamund.

'Oh, Ros'll make sure I do that,' Tony declared.

'Will she now?' The blue eyes glinted maliciously. 'My experience of young women is that they don't like attention diverted from themselves. Moreover, love can be detrimental to sport. I've known lads go to pieces in the throes of it.'

'Then you must have known some very weak-kneed specimens,' Rosamund returned with spirit.

He looked at her oddly. 'Perhaps they were,' he admitted. 'But there are degrees in love; perhaps your romance is not the intense variety that believes the world well lost for it?'

'Oh, that sort only occurs in books and plays,' Rosamund declared with the confidence of inexperience. 'Well balanced people preserve their sense of proportion.'

Adrian's mouth twitched with amusement at her naïveté and he said suavely: 'You disappoint me. After your exploit on the wall I imagined I'd got a modern Romeo and Juliet in my house.'

'What a thing to say!' Tony laughed uneasily, he knew his feelings for Rosamund lacked depth. 'I'm no Romeo and you must agree, sir, that the support of loved ones can be a great stimulus.'

'Could be,' Adrian conceded amiably. 'Another cup of tea, please, Miss Prescott.'

He doesn't believe we're in love at all, Rosamund thought as she poured it out, because we aren't obsessed with each other like those Italians, and she suddenly remembered that Romeo had climbed a wall to gain access to his beloved. But there the parallel ended. Tony had never stirred real passion in her; she had been quite content with their warm friendship and mutual liking, believing it was a more stable relationship than violent emotion. It occurred to her then that there were depths of feeling she had never plumbed and would never experience with him, whereas a man like Adrian Belmont could arouse sensations that would make the winning of international medals seem childish foolery by comparison. Was that what he had meant? She looked at him defiantly; she had divined from their first moment of meeting that Adrian Belmont was a disturbing personality, but she had no wish whatever to be drawn into any tempest of emotion that could wreck her placid existence. Tony suited her very well. Adrian's keen disconcerting eyes met hers as if he divined her thoughts and a little shiver ran down her spine. For a moment she fiercely regretted having come, intuitively aware that here was a menace to her tranquillity.

Subtly he guided the conversation to the subject of her own achievements and Tony let slip that she had won the All England Schools Championship.

'And you let it go at that?' Adrian demanded.

'Yes. I'm not a dedicated athlete.'

'What a waste!'

'Ros is only interested in *my* success,' Tony said with emphasis.

'How noble of her!' The look he gave Tony accompanying this exclamation was one of dislike, but Tony did not notice it. Rosamund did, and felt a prick of resentment. It was no business of Adrian Belmont's what she did with her talents ... or her life ... and if he imagined he could sow dissension between her and Tony upon this issue, he was very much mistaken. Yet perversely she wanted to awake his interest in her and she said carelessly:

'Of course you'd never condescend to coach a girl.'

Both men looked at her in surprise and Adrian laughed.

'I've never tried, but it might be an interesting experiment. Women can win gold medals too, and their events always arouse a good deal of public interest.'

'Have any of your protégés won an Olympic gold?' Rosamund asked.

He shook his head. 'Not yet, the Olympics only come every four years, and it isn't four years since,' his face darkened, 'I put myself literally out of the running.'

'They're to be held next year,' Tony remarked.

'That is so.' His eyes rested thoughtfully, not on Tony but on Rosamund.

They discussed the coming season, the events for which Tony should be entered and his chances in the various championships. Adrian entertained them with anecdotes about well-known sports personalities. He appeared to know many intimately, and though he was regarded as an authority on British athletics, he had refused to become a professional coach.

'I'm always ready to give advice when asked for it,' he told them, 'but I object to training all and sundry. I prefer to pick my own material.'

Tony flushed with pleasure. 'I feel honoured to be here.'

'Prove it by your performance,' was Adrian's uncompromising admonition. He went on to say how unfair it was that British athletes were not state-supported, but had to hold down a job while they were training, and Tony looked grim, knowing he might jeopardise his own occupation by giving so much time to athletics.

Mrs Grey came in to remove the tea things and Adrian looked at his watch.

'Back to the grind, my boy,' he said to Tony. 'I'll be out on the track in a few minutes.'

Tony looked doubtfully at Rosamund. 'How are you getting back, Ros?'

'Same way as I came, by bus from the village.' She hoped the last one had not gone.

'I'll run you home when I'm through,' Adrian offered. 'Meanwhile you'd better have a rest.' He looked with concern at her wan face.

'I couldn't let you . . .' she began, but he interrupted:

'Of course you can. You aren't fit to be jolted about in buses. After all, I was responsible for——' he grinned, 'the wall you fell off. Mrs Grey will take you to a room where you can lie down.'

Rosamund made no further protest, for her head was aching and she shrank from the walk to the village and the long bus ride. She said goodbye to Tony with slight constraint as Adrian was watching. He might have had the tact to leave them alone, she thought, but it did not seem to occur to him that she desired a more affectionate farewell than could be conducted in his presence. Nor did Tony respond to her wistful glances. He could have asked for a few moments together, but he did not; his mind was already on the running track and he went off whistling while Adrian spoke to his housekeeper. It was now dark, but Rosamund supposed the track was floodlit. She would have liked to see Tony in action, but again he had not suggested it.

The guest room into which she was shown was in front of the house, a big room luxuriously furnished. Mrs Grey turned on the small stove in the grate and drew back the eiderdown on the wide bed.

'Lie down, miss, and have a little sleep,' she suggested. 'Why not take your clothes off? I'll bring you a wrap and you'd be more comfortable. Or better still, have a bath.'

'That would be lovely,' Rosamund accepted gratefully. 'But will there be time?'

'Plenty, miss. The master's expecting you to stay to dinner.'

'But I couldn't impose . . .'

'You'd best do as he says,' Mrs Grey interrupted. 'He'll be busy outside for some time and he won't want to drive up to London without his dinner. Believe me, he'd have packed you off at once if he'd found you an imposition.'

That Rosamund was sure was true, but why did he want her to stay? He could not find her company enjoyable, but he was responsible for the wound in her head and might be trying to atone for that, and he might allow her to see Tony again before she left. She bathed in a bathroom adjoining the bedroom and slipped on the robe Mrs Grey had brought her. She lay down on the comfortable bed, switched off the bedside lamp and was almost immediately asleep. Waking in the strange room lit by the glow from the electric fire, she could not at first imagine where she was. Gradually the events of the day came back to her and she sat up with a gasp wondering what the time was. It felt like the middle of the night. Someone was knocking on the door and in answer to her 'Come in,' Mrs Grey opened it and switched on the light.

'Feeling better now, miss?' she enquired kindly.

'I think so.' Rosamund put her hand to her throbbing head.

'Cut painful? I'll get you some aspirin.' The house-keeper advanced into the room. 'Dinner will be ready in half an hour and I've pressed your clothes for you.' She laid the garments she carried on a chair. 'I looked in a while back, but you were sound asleep. The Master said I wasn't to disturb you.'

'Oh dear!' Rosamund scrambled off the bed and looked at her watch. It was nearly nine o'clock. 'You should have woken me.'

Mrs Grey laughed. 'That would have been against my orders.'

Rosamund dressed hurriedly and did what she could with her hair and face, which was not much, for she still looked washed out and the plaster was unsightly. She ran downstairs and stood hesitating in the hall, then made her way into the drawing room. Adrian was sitting in an armchair reading a sporting magazine, wearing a dark suit and looking immaculately groomed. The two dogs were lying on the hearthrug and raised their heads as she came in, though her feet had made no sound on the thick-piled carpet. Adrian noticed their action, saw her and dropped his magazine, rising to his feet.

'So the sleeping beauty has woken at last!'

'I'm sorry,' she faltered, wondering why she found it so hard to meet the quizzical blue eyes. 'I didn't mean to sleep so long.'

'I hoped it would do you good, but I can't say you look much better. Do you think you're fit to go home tonight?'

'Of course I am,' she declared hastily. 'I'm fine. I couldn't stay here.'

'Do you find my house so uncomfortable?'

'I didn't mean that, everything's lovely, but my parents would worry.'

'Really?' His voice held a note of mockery. 'I thought modern parents had to get used to their offspring being out all night.'

'I'm always in at a respectable hour,' she returned.

'Full marks for that, you appear to lead a disciplined life,' he said with approval. 'Shall we go and eat and we'll see how you feel after a meal.'

He moved towards her and with mock ceremony offered her his arm. Rosamund hung back.

'Isn't Tony coming?'

'Certainly not. I hope by now he's preparing for bed. Early hours are part of his routine.'

'So it's just you and me?'

'Just you and me.' His expression derided her nervousness. 'I assure you I don't bite.' Again he offered her his arm.

She put the tips of her fingers on his sleeve with a dreamlike sensation. This lovely house, its perfect appointments, did not seem real, nor did the flower-decorated table with its gleaming silver and crystal in the dining room into which he led her. As she seated herself in the chair he pulled out for her, she said wonderingly:

'Do you always dine like this when you're alone?'

'No, only when I have guests. I live mostly in the morning room, where you came in first, and eat off a tray when I'm alone.'

'You don't mean you've taken all this trouble just for me?'

'You're a guest, aren't you? And you did say it was your birthday. I thought a little festivity wouldn't be out of place.'

She was touched that he had remembered it.

A maid came in with the soup, saving her the necessity of a rejoinder. Rosamund was feeling a little overwhelmed; she could not understand why Adrian Belmont of all people was treating her with such consideration. The meal was excellent, the tomato soup followed by duck with orange sauce, sherry trifle, biscuits and cheese. They drank a hock and Rosamund, who was unused to wine, began to see her surroundings through a golden mist. Adrian, she decided, was wonderful, so handsome, generous and kind. How could she ever have entertained such hard thoughts about him? Under the mellowing influence of the wine, he told her a little about himself. His parents had died abroad in a cholera epidemic, and he, the only child and heir to the property, had been brought up by grandparents, now also dead. From a very early age he had excelled at sport, specialising in swimming and athletics until a motor accident had damaged his knee. All was told with whimsical understatement, defying her to offer sympathy. This her instinct warned her not to do, and in return she told him that she also was an only child, and her father too was very keen on sport though he had never got very far himself.

'He always encouraged me,' she said. 'You see, I'm not brainy or artistic and running was the only thing I was good at at school. I'm afraid he was disappointed when I gave up.'

'Have you given up?' he asked, looking at her intently. 'Don't you belong to the same club as Tony?'

'Yes, but I'm out of training.'

'In fact you're a lazy, stupid, unenterprising little girl,' he said, so pleasantly that she did not take in what he had said. 'What do you do with yourself that's more inspiring than running?'

'Lot's of things,' she told him vaguely, too contented with her dinner and her company to take offence. 'Dancing, reading, the cinema occasionally. Nothing special.'

It sounded an insipid list, though it was what most girls did. She wished she could lay claim to some outstanding talent or achievement to impress him. Yet did it matter what he thought of her? She was Tony's girlfriend and only this morning she had hated Adrian for keeping Tony away from her. Tony was her future, and, her tongue loosened by the wine, she went on:

'Of course, I'm expecting to get married and have a family.'

'The lucky man being Tony Bridges?'

'Of course. He *is* my boy-friend.'

'And won't be anything closer for a long while. Is he aware of your domestic plans?'

'Well . . .' she fingered her wine glass. Tony had not said anything definite about marriage, now she came to think of it. He had never been very definite about anything except his ambition to compete in the major games, but that had not seemed any real bar to their ultimate union.

'Athletes do have wives,' she said defiantly.

'True, but I gather young Bridges won't be in a position to support one for many a long year. His work is entirely second to his sport. Moreover, the more successful he is in that the bigger his ideas will become. Top athletes are celebrities. He'll go abroad and you'll be left behind— left behind in other ways as well. Your future with him is a very big gamble, my dear.'

That did penetrate her euphoria. She straightened herself in her chair and her amber eyes sparkled irefully.

'Are you trying to part us, Mr Belmont? You don't like

your protégés having other commitments, do you? You did your damnedest to keep me from seeing Tony. Let me tell you that though you know a lot about athletics, you don't really know anything about love, in spite of your cynical remarks. Tony and I mayn't seem to you to be crazy about each other, because we don't display our feelings, but he *does* love me and I . . .' She stopped, and a look of bewilderment gathered on her face. She had believed she loved Tony, but now she was assailed by sudden doubt. She knew what Adrian was warning her against, being not a grass but a track widow, the one who stayed at home and spent her life bolstering up her man's ego, for an athlete was every bit as vulnerable to defeat and failure as an actor or an artist. It meant surrendering her own personality to his, bearing with his fractious pre-race nerves, supporting him with adulation and having no life of her own. Could she do it? Did she want to do it?

'Do go on, Miss Prescott,' Adrian said suavely. 'You . . . what?'

She laughed, brushing aside the question. 'Anyway, running is a young man's sport. He'll retire eventually.'

'And you're prepared to wait until he does?'

'I don't suppose it'll be necessary,' she said sharply, resenting the question. 'It's getting late, Mr Belmont, shouldn't I be getting home?'

He glanced at his watch. 'Not so very late. We'll have coffee by the fire in the other room, and then I'll run you back, it won't take long.'

Back in the drawing room with the coffee table between them, she on the chesterfield, he in an armchair, before the crackling wood fire, a cosy intimacy enwrapped them. Rosamund was in no hurry to go home, though she knew it was getting very late; she would have liked to sit where she was all night, with Adrian sitting opposite to her almost as if he were her husband. She said mischievously:

'We might be Darby and Joan.'

'We might, but we aren't, we're too young to qualify. Certainly you are. All your life before you, Rosamund,' she thrilled as he used her first name. 'And there's so much you could do with it, if you don't persist in trying to waste it.'

She considered him out of wide-spaced amber eyes. He looked very serious as if her fate was a matter of great concern to him, his handsome head in strong relief against the white marble of the mantelpiece behind him. Again she was aware of a magnetic, almost a hypnotic force emanating from him.

'You think marrying Tony would be a waste?' she enquired.

'Frankly I do.'

'Then what would you suggest as an alternative?'

A sudden fire leaped in his eyes.

'An Olympic medal.'

She stared at him aghast. So this was what he had been leading up to, with his aspersions upon marriage with Tony! He had already told her she had squandered her potential. But if he thought she was going to embark upon a course of gruelling training towards an unattainable goal, he, not she, was the fool, for she knew her own limitations. She laughed scornfully.

'Mr Belmont, you've a one-track mind, but there's a difference between a school championship and a world one. Don't try to kid me I'd ever reach Olympic standard.'

'Nothing is impossible, if you've got the will to win.'

'I've heard that before, and I won't pretend that I don't enjoy running. Sometimes I've even thought of taking it up again seriously. But you mention the will to win, that's just what I lack, and you know it's a most important ingredient in an athlete's make-up. I'm short on determination.'

'That you're not, as you showed today.' He grinned wickedly. 'Neither ten-foot walls nor savage curs could keep you out.'

'That's different—I was motivated by love.'

'Nothing of the sort. You were motivated, as you put it, by your sheer dogged obstinacy and a desire to defeat me, and you succeeded in your objective at the price of that cut on your head.'

Rosamund coloured hotly, amazed at his perception.

'It seems to me,' he went on, 'you might find a more worthy object to expend your energy upon than a stolen meeting with a very ordinary young man.'

'He's not ordinary or you wouldn't have him here,' Rosamund pointed out. 'And no stolen meeting would have been necessary if you'd behaved like a rational human being and allowed me to visit him.'

'That's the grievance, isn't it? But consider, I've nearly a dozen lads training for a month here. If each of them was granted a free pass for a girl-friend, I'd have a dozen young females swarming all over the place every weekend, and not all of them would be as discreet as you are.' Again the blue eyes mocked her. 'Also I believe that self-restraint and self-denial are integral parts of the discipline of training. It does them no harm to be celibate for a few weeks.'

'Oh!' She flushed again. 'You make it sound as if I . . . if we . . . wanted . . . I mean, we wouldn't . . .'

'Not very coherent, are you, Miss Prescott? But I get your meaning. Of course you wouldn't, but others jump at every opportunity, so I don't provide the opportunity.' He lifted his head proudly. 'I'll permit no scandals at Belmont House.'

Rosamund dropped her eyes to her coffee cup, unwilling to admit that he had reason for his precautions. She knew enough of modern trends to understand that. Adrian leaned back in his chair watching her with lazy appreciation, noting the sculptured planes of her face, the bone formation that would never age, the droop of her well shaped mouth and her firm determined chin. The firelight painted ruddy lights in the deep gold of her hair, but more interesting to him were her long, straight legs with their clean bones and well-defined muscles, legs that would carry her to victory if his estimation of her was correct. He said:

'What you need is an incentive.'

Her eyes flashed up to his provocatively. 'Can you supply one?'

'Perhaps I could,' he told her softly. 'It depends how our ... er ... acquaintanceship develops.' She stared at him blankly; she had thought that would cease as from today. 'You being a woman, a personal one would appeal to you. Your Tony is far too egotistical to be interested in any career other than his own, you've already disappointed your father, but you might be reluctant to let down someone who had a firm belief in you, who had great faith in your ultimate victory.'

'But I don't know any such person.' She was bewildered. He was right to a certain degree. If someone she really cared about, Tony for instance, was set upon her success, she would have run herself to death to please him. Her father, after all, had been only half-hearted in his support.

'You do now,' he assured her. 'I mean myself.'

'What?'

He leaned forward and placed his hand over hers on the coffee tray. It was a well-shaped, long-fingered hand,

and an electric current seemed to flow from it into her veins, imbuing her with his vitality, but paralysing her will. She had a sudden premonition that he could make her do anything that he wanted.

'Rosamund, my dear,' his voice was low and persuasive, 'I want you to allow me to coach you and take your training in hand. I believe I can make you into a great athlete if you will permit me to do so. I know it's a long tough haul to reach the top, but I'll push you up there, I'll contrive to fire the ambition you say you lack. You say you disappointed your father—by the way, I'd like to meet him—but I'll ensure you don't disappoint me. Think of it, wouldn't you like to be someone in your own right, not just Tony Bridges' appendage? There's a satisfaction in achievement that's one of the prime joys of life. Besides, doesn't the Bible tell us we shouldn't hide our talents? You have one for running, and you ought to use it.'

He withdrew his hand, leaving her with a sense of deprivation, and leaned back saying carelessly: 'You'll have plenty of time for domesticity when you and Tony both retire.'

Rosamund looked at him, looked away and back to him again, drawn by a magnetism she could not resist. There was something mesmeric in those bright blue eyes. She should give him a flat denial, declare he had no right to interfere in her life, and that the last thing she wanted was the frequent contact with him coaching would entail —only she didn't. She became aware of a growing excitement, for Adrian Belmont exerted a fascination that drew her in spite of herself. Also she was flattered that he considered she was worth his attention, and who could say what their close association might lead to? Already her besotted brain began to weave fantasies around him. He was correct when he had suggested that he could stimulate her to efforts greater than any she had ever made, but she did not understand what he would get out of it.

'Why should you do all this for me?' she asked.

'Because your triumph will be my triumph. I can no longer compete myself, so I enjoy vicariously the success of others.'

An ambiguous reply that might have troubled her by its implications if she had had time to think, but she was swept away by the exhilaration of knowing that the great Adrian Belmont had selected her to win a medal for him.

'Oh, I would exert myself to the utmost to make you proud of me,' she cried, and became covered in confusion, realising that she had betrayed more than she had meant to do. The matter demanded calm consideration, perhaps even some bargaining before she capitulated.

Adrian gave her a long enigmatical look. He was not beyond using his physical attractions to gain his ends, and he was aware of the effect he was having upon this susceptible girl. But his smile was warm and sweet.

'Good girl, that's what I want.'

'But how ... and where? You can't have me here with the boys.'

'Definitely not with the boys, but they'll be leaving at the end of their course. After that I'll devote myself to you. You can come here at weekends, and there are other tracks. Your father can help—we'll make out a schedule for you.'

His face lit up with enthusiasm, and Rosamund knew a moment's pang. Was he seeing her only as a collection of bones and muscles that could be shaped and disciplined to move faster than any other female's anatomy? She wanted him to realise she was also a woman. But he might do that before very long, and in the meantime she must be obedient and docile.

'We must find out your full range,' he went on. 'I should say the four hundred metres or perhaps the eight hundred would be your best distances. With luck we'll get you into the W.A.A.A. Championship this summer.'

'You're going too fast,' Rosamund protested. 'The club doesn't think a lot of my form.'

'We've got to change all that.'

Rosamund descended from cloud cuckoo land with a bump as the practical details forced their way into her mind.

'I'm afraid it's all pipe dreams,' she said despondently. 'I've got my living to earn. The firm I work for won't see letting me have time off for meetings, and I might want to go abroad.'

'How unreasonable!'

'Not from their point of view. I work in a shop and my boss is more interested in my selling ability than my running time.'

'Are you a good saleswoman?'

She shook her head dolefully. 'The world's worst.'

'Then you must find another job.'

'It's not easy these days. I've no experience of anything else and I'm about adequate on the haberdashery counter.'

Adrian's eyes crinkled with laughter at these revelations.

'I'll find you something more congenial,' he promised, 'but that's only a minor detail.' He looked at his watch. 'I suppose we must see about getting you home. Are you sure you wouldn't prefer to spend the night here? You look tired.'

'I thought you wanted no scandal at Belmont House,' she said mischievously.

'What? Good heavens, girl, don't you think Mrs Grey is sufficient chaperone, to say nothing of the child? You've met Lucie?'

'Yes, a dear little thing.'

'I find her something of a menace, always where she shouldn't be.' He looked thoughtful. 'You're fond of children?'

'Oh, I am. Tony and I want a family.'

Tony. In her absorption in Adrian and his proposition, she had forgotten him.

'I don't know what he'll say about ... about me being trained by you,' she added.

'What's it to do with him? You don't imagine he'll be jealous?'

'Well ...' He might be, not of Adrian as a man, but of his interest in her. Adrian misunderstood her, he said with intense bitterness:

'No hale and hearty young man need be jealous of an old crock,' and limped to the door.

Rosamund had ceased to notice his disability, but she realised then that he was always conscious of it. She wanted to cry out that it did not matter, it did not diminish him, but wisely held her tongue, for she had already learnt that while he might refer to it himself, he would resent anyone else doing so.

# CHAPTER·THREE

IT was past eleven when Adrian set forth to take Rosamund back to the south London suburb where the Prescotts lived. He drove in silence through the spring night with her nearly asleep beside him. Half a century seemed to have elapsed since she had set out in the morning upon her quest, full of fury against the man who was driving her. What had happened since seemed so fantastic that she was inclined to think the latter part at least had been illusions created by her feverish brain, especially the dinner with Adrian and all that he had said to her, the result of the injury to her head. But his presence in the car must be real and he seemed solid enough. To assure herself of that she put out a tentative hand and laid it on his sleeve.

'What is it?' he demanded. 'Don't touch me while I'm driving.'

She hastily withdrew her hand.

'I'm sorry, I only wanted to make sure that you're real.'

That seemed to amuse him.

'Did you fear I was a spectre driving you to a hideous doom?' he asked banteringly. 'I'm solid, and heir to all the ills of the flesh. Your doom, we hope, will be far from hideous.' He became serious. 'Perhaps there's one thing I'd better mention, so you'll understand right from the word go. I'm not susceptible to girlish wiles, so don't be tempted to try them on. To me you're like the lad that I wish you were.'

'Thank you, Mr Belmont, for being so frank,' she returned coldly. 'I quite understand, and I hadn't any intention of wasting any girlish wiles, as you put it, on you. I keep them for those who appreciate them, though I'm not sure what they are. Our connection is a business one, and I prefer it that way.'

He need not have been so blunt, she thought; I suppose because I touched him he imagined I expected an erotic response, and she blushed fierily in the darkness at the mere suggestion. She did not suspect that his warning had been as much a reminder to himself as to her, for her wide-eyed appreciation of his home and the dinner he had provided for her had been very appealing.

Emboldened by the dark, and being intensely curious on that point, she enquired: 'Are there no women in your life, Mr Belmont?'

'Far too many,' he told her drily, 'but the only ones I really appreciate are those who minister to my comfort, in particular, Adela Grey. She's a treasure.'

'She seems a very nice woman,' Rosamund agreed, wondering about the 'far too many'. There were other comforts besides domestic ones that Mrs Grey could not supply. She hazarded again:

'You're not engaged?'

'Good God, no! I'm not a marrying man.'

'I see.' Her probing had got her nowhere, but he was unlikely to be expansive about his amours to her, and although athletics might be his ruling passion, she was sure he was not a man who lived like a monk.

'Inquisition over?' he asked pleasantly.

'I didn't mean to be impertinent,' she said quickly. 'I just wanted to be sure I don't tread upon anybody's corns. Other women mightn't understand you don't see me as a girl.'

Against her will there was a faint reproach in her last

sentence, and Adrian gave an exasperated sigh.

'Women!' he ejaculated. 'Rosamund Prescott, just forget you're one, to please me. In future I'll call you Ros like Tony does, it might be a boy's name.'

'Call me what you like,' she acceded frostily.

He was a mean wretch to tell her to forget her womanhood when he had got his own way by deliberately appealing to it. It was his charisma, not the lure of success, that had persuaded her. She was meditating revoking her acceptance and telling him to find some other stooge to win medals for him, when they reached the maze of suburban streets in her home district and she had to give all her attention to directing him. There would still be time to back out when he had reached her home and bade her farewell.

As they drew up at the kerb outside the house, she saw her father leaning over the small gate that gave admittance to their tiny strip of front garden.

'Ros?' he called. 'Is that you at last?'

She jumped out of the car, but in spite of his limp, Adrian reached her father first.

'Mr Prescott, isn't it?' he enquired. 'I must apologise for keeping your daughter out so late, but we've news for you which I'm sure will make you forgive us. Ros has decided to take up athletics again, and I'm going to train her.'

'I'm glad to hear that.' Paul Prescott sounded a little bewildered. 'But who may you be, sir?'

'Adrian Belmont. You may have heard of me.'

'*The* Mr Belmont? Of course I have, but how ... where?'

Adrian was not above enjoying his astonishment.

'If I may come in, we'll tell you all about it,' he said. 'Just let me lock up my car.'

Paul Prescott embraced his daughter. 'This is wonderful news! My darling, however did you work it? He must think you're good.'

Rosamund sighed. She could not draw back now. For good or ill her fate was linked with Adrian's.

She did not have an opportunity to inform Tony of her plans at once, for she did not see him alone for some time and she was oddly reluctant to do so. As a result possibly of Adrian's coaching, his times improved enormously and after doing well in the A.A.A. Championships he was selected to run in the International Games to be held in Sweden that summer. He had little time to spare and when they did meet he was too full of his successes to express much interest in her affairs. She did tell him that she had taken up running again seriously, and he was kindly patronising. She did not mention Adrian Belmont, not because of any wish to deceive him but because Tony was so supremely uninterested. He rarely visited the club and was unaware that she was becoming one of its best performers. Meanwhile she would have to endeavour to find a more sympathetic employer, for Adrian had planned a very full programme for her that summer, to fulfil which, if she were to carry it out, she would need more free time.

Rosamund went down to Belmont one Saturday afternoon when spring had given way to summer and the long trellis that shielded the running track from the rest of the grounds was a mass of climbing roses. By now she was familiar with the sports complex, the gymnasium, swimming pool, canteen and the bunkhouse that had been built to accommodate Adrian's protégés, and also the circle of track laid down for their practice runs. On that day the complex was deserted.

Rosamund had been practising starting, the leap forward from the blocks that was so important. Adrian had worked her hard, and feeling hot and sweaty, she was thinking longingly of the cool shower installed in the complex, when he told her curtly:

'Wait a minute, I've something to say to you.'

As it was a sunny June day, she had no need of track suit or sweater, and picking up her blocks, she went to join him where he lay on the grass under a tree, the dogs beside him. He watched her approach, with his chin supported on cupped hands—a slim graceful figure, her hair gilded by the sun, her long legs and arms delicately tanned—with a curious enmity in his eyes, as if he were envying her her youth and unblemished limbs. Rosamund caught his expression and felt her heart sink. There were times when she thought Adrian actually disliked her, though there seemed to be no reason for his antipathy except that she was a girl and he feared her feminine temperament might defeat his plans for her. That was a quite unwarrantable suspicion, for she was showing herself as dedicated to his aims as any boy could have done, although to be completely honest, she would not have been so keen if it were not for his stimulus. She had said she wanted to make him proud of her and to do that she would have to climb to the top of the tree, however much it cost her in expenditure of energy and time. If he dropped her, she would lose her new-found interest in running, and possibly he knew that it was the personal motive which drove her and that was what annoyed him.

He was wearing trousers and a singlet—he never wore shorts because of the injury to his knee—and looked attractive, his bared arms and neck the colour of teak, his eyes by contrast startlingly blue in his dark face. His body was hard and lean, for he exercised regularly in the gym when nobody was about, and he was able to ride. Rosamund had occasionally glimpsed him galloping across the park.

The dogs, lying flat on their sides because of the heat, flapped languid tails at her approach. They knew her now.

'Sit down,' Adrian said sharply. 'I hate people hovering over me.'

Meekly she subsided on to the grass at a little distance from him and began to pluck idly at a daisy plant in the herbage. She was always afraid his keen glance might surprise too much in her eyes, so she kept them averted, for during these weeks of intimacy his attraction for her had grown, not lessened. Though when she was actually working she lost her self-consciousness, while concentrating upon her efforts, in more intimate moments, she became almost painfully aware of him.

'You've improved a lot,' he told her, and she flushed, for words of praise were rare from him. 'But you're tired, much too tired. That damn shop of yours takes too big a toll of your energy.'

'It can't be helped.'

'It must be helped, and I think I have the solution.' He reached over and absently began to caress Roland's ears. The dog thumped his tail appreciatively. 'Adela is finding her chores too much for her. Most of the help we have in the house comes in daily and isn't very dependable. Last week I gave two dinner parties to members of foreign sports associations, and the child made herself a nuisance. She had croup or some such.'

'Poor little thing, she couldn't help that,' declared Rosamund, who had had an account of the occurrence from Lucie's grandmother.

'Granted, but she played havoc with my carefully

planned arrangements.' He rolled on his back, staring up into the branches of the tree above him. 'Would you consider looking after her? It would release Adela for other duties, and I believe you're fond of the brat.'

Rosamund relinquished her attentions to the daisy and stared at him.

'But ... but I should have to live here.'

He turned his head to look at her, his eyes azure slits between his narrowed lids, then as if the sight of her glowing youth was too much for him, he closed them.

'Would that be too much of a hardship?' he asked sarcastically. 'You know that although isolated, we've got all the mod cons. If the brat isn't too exigent you could also give Adela a hand when we're entertaining, if it isn't beneath your dignity.'

'I'd be glad to do it ... but ...'

'I'd pay you what you're earning now,' he cut in. 'Perhaps a bit more.'

'That wouldn't be fair. I mean, I'd get my keep, shouldn't I? And the duties don't sound arduous.'

'They aren't, but that's the point. You'll be able to give more time to training.' He opened his eyes and grinned at her. 'Out on the track at six in the morning. And you'll have all the free time you need to attend sports meetings. Don't forget, ours is a joint undertaking, and I'm the judge of what you're worth.'

Rosamund was silent, clasping and unclasping her hands. She always had a few words with Lucie when she came to Belmont and she had become fond of the child. The house was a luxurious place in which to live and the employment offered to her would be a sinecure after the long hours in the shop, nor did she think her parents would raise any objection; they were worried that she was doing too much. But if she came to live at Belmont House

she would be completely and utterly under the domina-
tion of its master. Already he occupied her thoughts to
the point of obsession, and theirs was becoming a sort of
Svengali–Trilby relationship. He was building her up to
become a great athlete, but scorned her femininity, and
sometimes it was a relief to get away from him and escape
from his constant criticisms. But the hours apart from
him were empty and she only lived for their next meeting. If she lived in his house there would be no escape
from him and she would end up completely his slave.

Adrian frowned impatiently. 'Why are you hesitating?
Don't you think it would be the solution of all our problems?'

All but one, the one she did not want to have to admit.

'It seems quite a good idea,' she agreed. Then a way
out suddenly occurred to her. 'I don't think Tony would
like it, and he has a right to be consulted.'

He sat up abruptly, blue eyes blazing. 'Hell's bells,
haven't you forgotten that nonsense?'

'It isn't nonsense! I'm very attached to Tony . . .'

'Then the sooner you unattach yourself the better. Are
you sure he hasn't forgotten you?'

Sadly she reflected that Tony was well on the way to
doing just that, but he had no other girl-friend and she
had vaguely assumed that when he was less busy at the
end of the season they would take up the threads where
they had left off, but she thought he would not approve of
her living at Belmont, and she had no intention of allowing Adrian to know she had doubts about the durability
of their connection.

'I'm quite sure he hasn't,' she declared. 'I see him
from time to time and he knows I'm very interested in his
career.'

The blue eyes met hers with piercing intensity.

'And that's all you're interested in?'

'Of course not. Oh, if you weren't so inhuman you wouldn't ask such stupid questions!'

Adrian chuckled softly. 'So you think I'm inhuman, Miss Ros? Impervious to male weakness, perhaps?'

A perverse impulse caused her to reply: 'You act like that towards me.'

'Meaning I haven't made a pass at you?' Rosamund's face flamed and she hurriedly turned away her head. 'My dear girl, haven't I explained that anything like that would be fatal to your chances? But that's always the way with women, they insist upon introducing emotional complications.'

Rosamund sprang to her feet, stung by the implication, which was uncomfortably near the truth.

'Can't you take a joke?' she asked stormily. 'I was only teasing. I look upon you as a sort of schoolmaster, and the last person I'd ever fall for—you're far too tyrannical!' Adrian blinked, and his face became expressionless. 'Besides, we were talking about Tony,' she went on, 'he's nearer my age and ... and ...'

'Isn't maimed,' Adrian completed her sentence, while she groped for the right word, which certainly was not that. His mouth twisted bitterly and he lay back on the grass. 'Okay, Ros, calm down, you look like an angry dryad—weren't they the creatures that haunted woodlands? Now I'm questioning *your* humanity.' He was talking at random, as if to conceal what he was thinking. 'Do I take it that subject to Tony Bridges' approval you'll accept my offer?'

Rosamund's spurt of passion had died away at his reference to his lame leg. He was inordinately sensitive about it, and she wondered if it could really cause him to feel inferior to boys like Tony. To her mind there was no comparison between them, and the advantages were all on Adrian's side, but after her declaration of her indifference towards him she dared not say anything reassuring for fear of being misunderstood.

'If he agrees I will,' she said, confident that Tony would object and thus save her the necessity of making a decision. He was inclined to think he had proprietorial rights in Belmont and Adrian since he had trained there.

But Tony, to her dismay and surprise, did not mind in the least.

'It'll be a change from the shop,' he said carelessly. 'That is if you like looking after kids—but don't let Belmont take advantage of your good nature. Those swell dames he has down from London take a lot of waiting upon and you don't want to degenerate into a slavey.'

'Does he have smart ladies from London to stay?'

'Lord, yes, you don't imagine he's a hermit? He had a crowd down one weekend when I was there. Of course we weren't allowed to fraternise, but they came down to the pool one evening and we got a squint at them. I don't know where he picks them up, they looked like actresses or models. The men with them didn't look like athletes, though they may have been ex-ones.'

This information came as a surprise to Rosamund, who had imagined that Adrian in private life existed in isolated seclusion. Also it was extremely unpalatable. It seemed Adrian consoled himself for his mishap among fast society. She must seem gauche and unsophisticated to him, so it was easy for him to maintain an impersonal relationship when he had a bevy of lovelies to choose from when he was feeling amorous. Far from being inhuman, he was rather too much so.

'So you won't mind if I go to live there?' she queried.

Tony shrugged his shoulders. 'Suit yourself.'

Stung by his lack of interest, she asked sweetly:

'You don't think I'll be corrupted by Belmont's slick friends?'

'You won't mingle with them, my darling. You're going there to work, aren't you?'

She persisted, 'I thought you might be jealous.'

'Of whom? You and Belmont?' he laughed merrily. 'He may condescend to coach you occasionally, but he's not attracted by young girls, he likes 'em mature and sophisticated. You aren't smitten with him, are you? Surely he isn't your type?'

'Definitely not,' she said with emphasis, wincing inwardly at Tony's description of Adrian's preferences. 'He's a lot older than I am anyway, and I like *young* men.' She gave him a coy look.

'Of course you do,' Tony returned, patting her shoulder. 'And you'll soon get tired of this running craze, you did before when you left school. It keeps you fit and it's something to do, but you're not the sort to become dedicated.'

His condescension was so irritating that Rosamund would have liked to kick him, but she controlled the sharp words upon her lips. Least of all to Tony did she want to betray her feelings towards Adrian, nor to confide in him her new ambitions which might come to nothing after all. It was true she had lost interest in athletics when she left school, but this time she meant to persevere until she had achieved something worth having.

It was trying to have to swallow her pride and admit to Adrian that Tony had raised no objection to his plans; it would confirm his belief that Tony was no longer interested in her, but she was too honest to pretend otherwise.

Adrian smiled satirically when she told him.

'I'm gratified that Bridges is ready to throw his ewe lamb into the maw of the wolf. Is he naïvely trusting, or doesn't he care?'

'I shall ignore that remark,' Rosamund told him with dignity. 'It's uncalled-for, but I believe you can't help making snide comments.'

'Perfectly true, it's my nasty, twisted nature,' he returned. 'But since you understand me so well, you know what to expect when you come to work for me.'

Seeing his derisive smile, Rosamund felt a sudden qualm.

'But I haven't said . . .'

'Oh yes, you have. You promised that if your Tony agreed you would come.'

'Then I can't go back on my word,' Rosamund conceded, inwardly excited by the prospect of life at Belmont House. Her doubts were further dispelled by Mrs Grey's delight at her news.

'The poor bairn often feels neglected,' she said. 'I've so much to see to, what help we have has to be supervised. Besides, she needs someone young to take charge of her. I can't trust the maids.'

They were in the housekeeper's room and thought they were alone, but Lucie crawled out from under the table where she had been playing, nodding her head of dark curls.

'Granny always says go and play with your dolls and don't bother me.'

'Oh, child, I didn't know you were there,' Mrs Grey exclaimed. 'It's not true, I only say that when I'm extra busy.'

'You always are extra busy,' Lucie accused her. She looked up at Rosamund. 'You're the running lady, isn't you? Can I watch you run?'

'If you like,' Rosamund told her, hoping Adrian would tolerate the child's presence. After all, she was supposed to be looking after her.

He did. 'She'll get tired of it long before you do,' he told her. 'But she can always play with the dogs. They'll not let her come to any harm.'

'What well trained dogs!'

'As I told you before, all my dependants are well trained.'

'Including me?' she asked pertly.

'Oh, you're learning to come to heel quite nicely,' he declared with a crooked grin.

Rosamund's life settled down into a routine where athletics were given priority. She was accommodated in a pleasant bedroom next to Lucie's at the side of the house. Mrs Grey's was also in that wing and they had their own bathroom. Downstairs the housekeeper's room next to the kitchen was where they sat, ate and Lucie played. Rosamund's duties were light, mainly keeping Lucie amused, taking her for walks, bathing her and putting her to bed, for at that time Mrs Grey was usually occupied with preparing dinner. She also gave her some preliminary lessons that were more like games. The little girl would be going to school after Christmas.

Early morning and late evening she was out on the track following the schedule Adrian had drawn up for her, which included exercises in the gym to increase stamina and test her endurance.

As he had no other pupils for Rosamund to run against, Adrian utilised his dogs, an idea inspired by her first race with one of them. The intelligent creatures soon understood his commands, 'Go—sprint—jog!' They sprinted with alacrity but were reluctant to slacken pace. They did give Rosamund some competition and she shared their sheer physical joy in running; they made a charming trio, the long-legged golden-haired girl and her two red-coated attendants, but there was only Adrian to enjoy it. When the animals had had enough they flopped panting by the track side, while Rosamund jogged steadily on, until they were rested, when Adrian would call to them to rejoin her, and they would bound beside her, pacing her towards the finishing line.

Unfortunately an enterprising local reporter got wind of these proceedings and an article appeared in the local press headed 'World-Renowned Coach trains his Athletes to Compete with Dogs,' much to Adrian's annoyance. This resulted in a visit from the R.S.P.C.A. inspector alerted by an old woman in the village, to his further indignation. Roland and Oliver treated him with aloof disdain, but they were obviously in splendid condition and Rosamund supported her employer when he declared they only 'played games together,' so the man apologised and departed. The reporter had tried hard to obtain a photograph to substantiate his article, seeking to force an entry during training sessions, but he was unsuccessful.

'He's not as smart as you were,' Adrian told Rosamund with his crooked smile. 'But then he isn't motivated by love.'

He never missed an opportunity to tease her about her love for Tony, and she played up to him, pretending a greater affection than she really felt. Vaguely she felt Tony was a bulwark against a new feeling stirring in her heart, an emotion she did not want to examine too closely.

At weekends she ran in club events and occasionally at county meetings. When she had a free Sunday she went home. Her father was delighted that she was making pro-

gress under the auspices of such a famous athlete and her
mother was pleased that she was mixing with 'nice
people', though actually she did not do any mixing. When
Adrian had a house party, he became invisible and Rosamund helped Mrs Grey, who was also the cook, to pre-
pare the extra meals.

Sometimes she took Lucie home with her and Mrs
Prescott made much of the child, not minding when Lucie
tactlessly commented upon the smallness of the Prescott
house.

'My home's ever so big and we've a 'normous garden.
You've got hardly any garden at all.'

Rosamund wondered if Adrian's kindness had not
been misplaced. Lucie was developing grandiose ideas
and she was only at Belmont House on sufferance, but
Adela told her:

'She'll understand when she's older, and the Master
did say she was to consider this house her home. He'll always look after her. He believes she has a right to be
here.'

A remark that caused Rosamund to ponder, refusing to
accept its obvious significance. She hoped Adela was not
over-confident. If Adrian ever married his wife might
not approve of Lucie having the freedom she now enjoyed, for she roamed all over the house, even invading
the master's privacy, and he treated her with indulgent
kindness.

'Such a pity he's none of his own,' Adela remarked
more than once. 'Ah well, there's time yet, though I don't
think any of the brazen bits he seems to favour would
make him a good wife.'

'Perhaps that's why he hasn't married one of them,'
Rosamund suggested, secretly glad that Adrian did not
appear to have any serious intentions towards anyone.

Since she had come to live at Belmont House, his manner towards her was coldly formal, and on the track he was very much the exacting coach; there were no more of the intimate conversations they had once enjoyed, though upon reflection they had been more like sparring matches. But sometimes she would catch his eyes upon her with an enigmatical expression which she could not read, but which made her heart beat faster, and she would hope wildly that perhaps he did sometimes see her as a girl after all.

One June evening, when he had a party staying at the house and she did not expect to see him, he came out to the track accompanied by two supercilious young ladies wearing smart track suits and running shoes, who glanced at Rosamund contemptuously. She had just stripped off her sweater and felt naked and vulnerable in her vest and shorts against their elegance.

'I've brought a little competition for you, Ros,' Adrian explained. 'These two charming ladies,' he threw the two girls a satirical look, 'have agreed to run with you tonight. They aren't novices, so you'd better do your best.'

Amid much laughter and banter they took off their suits. Adrian gave them each their positions and took out his stopwatch.

'Two laps,' he decreed. 'We've no tape, but the first over the finishing line ...' this was marked in white paint '... will of course be the winner.'

He had not introduced his friends, but later Rosamund was to discover one of them was an international champion, and it was obvious they had agreed to the exercise to humour their host and were not expecting any serious competition. Rosamund resolved she would beat them if it killed her, their scorn being the spur she needed to exert herself to the limit. She settled down to her blocks, as Adrian produced the starter's pistol he had brought with him. At the signal she was off like an arrow, and soon realised she was up against fierce competition and would do well to conserve her strength for the final spurt. Surrendering the lead, she allowed them to pass her but kept close at their heels throughout the first lap, and they, believing she could not catch them, were not hurrying. On the second lap she drew alongside, sensing their surprise that she was still there. The less expert of the pair dropped behind and Rosamund was running neck and neck with the other one. She saw Adrian's figure beside the track, the white line, and shot ahead of the girl beside her, finishing a good two yards ahead of her.

'Well done,' Adrian said softly, as she staggered to the edge of the track, 'but your time during the first lap was much too slow. You should have pushed them more.'

The girl she had just beaten came up to them. 'Adrian, you beast!' she exclaimed. 'You might have warned me.' She gave Rosamund an inimical look. 'I didn't expect her to be able to run like that.'

'In sport you must always be prepared for the unexpected,' he returned imperturbably.

'But who is she?' the second girl demanded. 'I was told she was Lucie's nursemaid.' Her dark eyes showed an unwilling respect.

'Unfortunately yes, since British athletes have to have a job, because our government doesn't support them,' Adrian pointed out. 'Ros, put on your sweater before you take cold. What about a drink to celebrate your victory?'

Rosamund excused herself, she did not want to accompany him and his friends into the house.

'I still have some exercises to do, according to my schedule,' she reminded him.

'You've done enough for tonight,' he told her.

'I could do with a drink,' one of the girls said plaintively, and the other one addressed Rosamund for the first time.

'Is our Adrian such a slave-driver?'

'The plantation overseers had nothing on him,' Rosamund confirmed, her eyes sparkling.

'Poor you,' the girl said casually, and Adrian laughed.

'Some workers only respond to the whip and the spur,' he declared. 'You've been spurred tonight, Ros, and you've surpassed my expectations.' His eyes flickered over her, alight with blue flame. 'Well, if you won't drink with us, please excuse us, we've got neighbours coming in for cards, but don't do any more tonight.'

Rosamund watched them go wistfully, Adrian with a girl hanging on to either arm while one of the dogs proudly carried his stick. If he had pressed his invitation she would have gone with them, but he had not done so and he did not really wish for her company. Their gay laughter floated back to her, borne on the slight breeze; she was not in their class, but for all that she divined that Adrian secretly despised them. Yet he treated them with careless intimacy, while to her he had become frigid. Even his words to her tonight when she had come victorious off the track had been qualified.

Despondently she picked up her blocks and sweater and reluctantly moved towards the house. She would spend the evening alone with Mrs Grey in the housekeeper's room while in the drawing room they would be laughing and joking, including a few cracks perhaps at the nursemaid who had exhibited such unexpected prowess. Adrian would not defend her, since he would have no wish to reveal to that frivolous company his ambitions for her.

She stopped and looked back at the wide spaces of the park; they seemed to beckon to her. The coming of night always brought about a resurgence of energy and new vigour pulsed through her limbs. She dropped her burden, tossed back her hair and began to run, seeking release from her troubled thoughts in the sheer primitive delight in her own swiftness.

Dusk was gathering under the trees, but above her head the sky was a clear blue shading to mauve in the west where the glowing colours of the sunset still lingered. A first star, forerunner of its fellows, shone in the east with the steadiness that proclaimed it was a planet. My star, Rosamund thought exultantly, and it's rising. She ran on, not on the track but over the dew-drenched grass, threading between the trees, a white-limbed nymph flitting through the dusk. So had Daphne fled from Apollo, Syrinx from Pan, but Rosamund ran from her own thoughts, the recollection of those two amorous girls hanging on Adrian's arms and the dark sexual jealousy that had raised its ugly head while she watched them.

She circled the park, as the moon rose over the trees, a great golden orb. An owl hooted, then swooped ahead of her on silent wings—a barn owl, a white ghost in the half light. She did not see the dark figure emerging from the shadow of a stand of trees to intercept her and ran straight into its arms.

'I told you not to do any more tonight.' But he did not release her. Her face was ivory in the wan light, her hair silver, her eyes dark pools of mystery. Her heart was throbbing with the violent exercise and he put one hand over her breast as if to still its tumult.

'Are you crazy?' he asked, but his voice was soft.

'Yes, quite crazy.' She laughed exultantly. 'I feel invincible tonight, and the moon looks like a gold medal, the medal I'm going to win. Oh, Adrian, do you think I've a chance of it?'

In her wild mood she had used his name, though she was usually careful to address him formally.

'Damn all medals,' he said roughly, 'they can't compensate for ... everything.'

She became aware that he was still holding her and made a movement to withdraw herself.

'No, you don't,' he tightened his clasp. 'Not until that heart of yours has ceased to race. I've caught you and I'll keep you, you little wild thing. Now just calm down.'

But her heart was beating faster because of his proximity, and she murmured with a catch in her breath:

'I was excited by my win.'

He chuckled throatily. 'That girl was ...' and he mentioned a well-known name. 'You shook her, my sweet.'

Suddenly he bent his head and his lips touched hers. Instantly she took fire, her arms crept round his neck and she clung to him while his mouth became more demanding. Her slim palpitating body in his arms excited him, and he crushed her closer, moulding her figure into his. They stood interlocked, lost to time and place. Adrian's hard lean body, pressed against hers, his seeking mouth, and the sensations he was arousing in her, swamped all coherent thought in Rosamund's mind; she was swept by rapture.

Again the owl hooted and a bat flitted across the face of the moon. The melancholy sound broke the spell that enmeshed them, and Adrian almost violently pushed her away.

'Moon madness,' he ejaculated, but his voice was unsteady. He took out his handkerchief and wiped his face while Rosamund stood quivering, wondering what had happened and what would come next. When he spoke again his voice was curt and clipped.

'Where's your sweater? You'll catch a chill. Here . . .' He peeled off his jacket and swung it over her shoulders. It was his dinner jacket, lined with silk, and smelt of talc and shaving lotion. Rosamund saw he was looking for his stick which he had dropped when she ran into his arms. It was at her feet. She picked it up and handed it to him.

'Thanks,' he said harshly, 'a timely reminder that I'm a cripple.' She made a small sound of dissent, but he ignored it.

'Now will you obey orders and go indoors?' he went on. 'My guests will wonder where I am.'

She walked beside him meekly, hanging her head. The moon had turned to silver and decreased in size as it rode up the sky. The house ahead of them was ablaze with lights from the uncurtained lower windows.

'I didn't expect to meet you in the park,' Rosamund said as if to excuse herself.

'That was obvious. I came out for a breather between rubbers. I never thought I'd meet Diana hunting in the woods.'

'I wasn't hunting.' She noticed an acid note in his voice.

'Don't spoil my classical metaphor. Are you sure you weren't looking for Endymion?'

'Who on earth was he?'

'Diana's, or Artemis as the Greeks call her, lover. She came upon him sleeping in the woods and was so taken with him she had him wafted to Olympus where he slept forever dreaming of her. Quite a chaste affair compared with most of those legends.'

Rosamund wondered if this was an oblique way of

hinting that she had had an assignment with someone in the park.

'I wasn't looking for a lover,' she said crossly, 'if that's what you're getting at, and I met ... you.'

'And I acted like a satyr, but a half-naked girl running into my arms on a night like this was too much for my self-control. You see, I'm human after all.'

'I only wish you'd be human a bit more often.'

He stopped and looked at her sternly.

'Please Ros, none of the provocative stuff. What happened was ... unfortunate, and I'll be obliged if you forget it. You caught me off guard, but it shan't happen again. You're no icicle, but I'm afraid you'll have to do without lovers until you pass beyond my jurisdiction. As I've said so often, you need all your concentration for your sport.'

He spoke harshly and though he had been more to blame for what had occurred than herself, she checked her rising indignation, for she was intuitively aware that he was blaming himself bitterly for his lapse, and that was all it had been on his part, an amorous impulse aroused by the magic of the night and a woman in his arms. She swallowed convulsively, for it was a bitter pill to swallow, and walked on in silence towards the side door which she used in preference to the stately front entrance.

He followed her, and when they reached it, Rosamund slipped off his jacket and handed it to him.

'I ... I'm sorry.' She did not know for what she was apologising, but she was dimly aware that something rather beautiful had been born that night and that Adrian had killed it with his cruel cynicism. All rubbish and wishful thinking, but if only he had been ... different.

'Think no more of it.' He shrugged into his coat which

she held for him. 'Incidentally, I hope to enter you for the
W.A.A.A. Championships in July, at the Crystal Palace.
Maybe I'll need to pull a few strings, but I'll manage it.
It's time my duckling turned into a swan, and I know
you won't let me down.'

'That'll be wonderful,' she told him, trying to infuse
enthusiasm into her voice. At that moment she did not
care if she never ran again.

He touched her cheek lightly with his forefinger and
smiled.

'That'll give you something to dream about tonight. Go
and have a shower. Goodnight.'

But it was not of future triumphs that Rosamund
dreamed that night, but of Adrian's arms and Adrian's
kisses.

# CHAPTER FOUR

AT the Crystal Palace Rosamund won the final of the four hundred metres in record time and the eyes of the athletic world began to turn in her direction. Britain had little outstanding talent that year among its feminine runners, and the long-legged, red-haired girl with her muscles of steel appealed to the popular imagination. For the rest of the season her life increased its tempo, and the press began to notice her.

Adrian Belmont guarded her as zealously as a duenna, cracking down on public appearances and social invitations. He managed her business, arranged her fixtures and wafted her back to the seclusion of Belmont House between her competitions. It began to be whispered that he was hoping she would make the Olympic team next year.

Adrian was himself something of a legend, and a target for female eyes. He was so good-looking, wealthy and apparently a confirmed bachelor. Rumours began to circulate that he was at last entangled in a romance and its heroine was the unknown athlete he had suddenly produced. But none of these rumours reached Rosamund and if Adrian heard them he treated them with disdain.

Winter put an end to the sports season except for a few indoor events in which Rosamund did not participate, though she continued assiduously with her training. Parties were ruled out, rarely now were guests invited to the house. But though he watched over her so carefully, Adrian maintained his aloof attitude towards her. Never again did he betray any emotion, though as the episode in the park receded he became more friendly in a casual, fraternal manner. Rosamund thought she understood his feelings, or lack of feelings, perfectly. They were working for a mutual aim, the Olympic team, and so long as she ordered her life as he directed, he approved of her. This indifference of his maddened her to the point of rebellion, but there was nothing she could do about it. If she disappointed him he would wash his hands of her and look for another puppet to do his bidding. For that was all she was to him, a marionette, answering to the pull of the strings as he directed them. He would be furious if she displayed any emotion, though she knew he would not be surprised if she did. He was contemptuous of women and was watching for any signs of weakness which he would attribute to her sex's instability; so that she went through her daily routine with grim determination, resolved to prove herself completely dedicated to running. She found it hard going, for she had come to realise to her dismay and against her will that she had fallen in love with her stern mentor. He was the only man who counted in her life, and if he inadvertently touched her he set all her nerves tingling. She would not admit even to herself that it *was* love, though it might be infatuation. It was more like a fixation, an obsession which turned all her thoughts in his direction, and since there seemed no hope that he would ever reciprocate, it caused her much unhappiness.

Christmas approached, and to Rosamund's surprise Adrian was preparing to make a big thing of it. She told him that her parents would expect her to spend it at home, half hoping that he would forbid the visit, for she did not want to go, but he agreed at once. Of course they would want her at home, Christmas was a home festival, a gathering of the clans.

'Only there are no members of the Belmont clan to congregate,' he told her, 'except for some distant cousins with whom I've not kept up. But Adela and Lucie will want to celebrate it, and we must have a tree and all the trimmings for the child. As for yourself, a break will do you good, prevent you from becoming stale.'

She was to go on Christmas Eve and return on the day after Boxing Day.

'I'm taking Lucie to the pantomime in the afternoon,' he told her, to her astonishment; Adrian and pantomimes seemed incongruous. 'We'll pick you up in the afternoon on the way home. On the next evening I'm giving a small party, and I want you to be present at it.'

'Is that really necessary?' she asked doubtfully, for if the party was to include some of Adrian's girl-friends, she hated having to watch him flirting with them. She knew they meant nothing to him, but since he never favoured her with any gallantries, their easy familiarity made her feel excluded, and there was always the dread that one of them would turn out to be someone special. She despised herself for being jealous, but recognised it was an inevitable part of being in love—if she were in love.

'I mean ... it's awfully good of you to ask me,' she went on, 'I do appreciate it, but I'd feel out of it among all your smart friends.'

'There won't be very many, and I'll pick friendly ones. You deserve a little fun.' He pinched her cheek with careless casualness. 'All work and no play makes Jack a dull boy, and that applies to Jill too. I don't suppose your family reunion will be madly exciting.'

That would be true. Her father would put her through a catechism about her running performances and her mother be engrossed in preparing meals which they would eat in front of the television. Well, she would only be with them for three nights, and surely she could put up with the monotony with good grace for their sakes. Hitherto she had been content with their companionship, but now she knew her thoughts would be turning towards Belmont House all the time, wondering what was happening there.

She went up to town one afternoon to do her Christmas shopping, travelling by bus. Adrian had raised no objection. Lucie wanted a big, big doll. Though she had an extensive collection, she was always eager for one more. Mrs Grey, she had discovered, loved good scent. Rosamund was ready to spend the salary she always felt she did not really earn upon them and her friends and relatives. There was one other person she wanted to remember, but what could she buy for Adrian, who had everything? In the end she chose a bronze statuette of two runners. The slim graceful figures were so well modelled they seemed only temporarily frozen into immobility and might suddenly leap forward. It was very expensive and cost more than all her other presents put together.

A giant fir tree was brought into the hall and installed in one corner of it. On the morning of Christmas Eve Rosamund helped to dress it, before she left for home in the afternoon. There were boxes of tinsel strings and blown glass ornaments and a fairy doll to be fixed on the top of it. Adrian came in to attend to the lighting and she asked him to put the doll in position. Lucie had been sent to play with little friends at the Vicarage while all this was being done. They would come back with her to tea, when the tree would be shown to them in all its glory. Rosamund regretted that she would not be there to witness the child's delight. Adrian climbed up a step-ladder and attached the glittering figure to the topmost branch, Rosamund steadying the ladder while he performed this operation. The doll stared at him out of round blue eyes set in a waxen face surrounded by a mass of yellow curls. He came down again, dusting his fingers against his pants.

'She's not for distribution,' he said, glancing up at his handiwork. 'I mean, Lucie can't have her or the other children will be jealous. We'll keep her with the decorations for next year.'

Next year—Rosamund caught her breath. By then the Olympics would be over and what would have become of her? One thing was certain, whether she did well or ill, her connection with Adrian would have been severed. It was not certain she would be selected by any means, but Adrian was sure that she would be. Four years was too long to wait for her next chance and he was pinning all his hopes upon next summer.

She glanced at his dark face as he stared up at the doll and her heart swelled within her. How could she live parted from him? He wore a black turtleneck sweater with dark trousers and looked lithe and a little demonic, his chiselled profile shown up by the dark panelling of the hall. Mrs Grey had left them to perform some duty and Adrian seemed to have no thought for anything except the doll.

'Vapid expression she's got, hasn't she?' he remarked. 'If she's got any expression at all. I've known quite a number of girls like her—empty-faced and empty-headed for all their prettiness. God, what bores they are!'

'Don't you like pretty blondes?' Rosamund asked provocatively. 'And I've always understood men preferred empty-headed girls, the clever ones put them off.'

He removed his gaze from the doll to look at her. She

too wore a dark sweater, and she became conscious that she was wearing no make-up, and her hair was tousled from her efforts with the tree. She must be looking very unglamorous compared with the fairy beauty, but Adrian more often than not saw her so, when she came off the track.

'I don't like bluestockings,' he admitted. 'They're so obsessed with their own brilliance that they're worse bores than the stupid ones. Besides, intellectual women so often dress atrociously. A woman should be decorative and intelligent enough not to flaunt either her physical or mental endowments.'

'A typical masculine viewpoint,' Rosamund said disdainfully, thinking sadly that she had nothing to flaunt, except a turn of speed which was hardly a feminine attribute.

'Not at all. I don't know how women react to each other, not very charitably from what I've noticed, but my remarks can apply to men as well as girls.'

'But men don't need to be decorative.'

'So they seem to think, from the way they dress nowadays. Tell me, Ros, would you like me to grow my hair to my shoulders, sport an untidy beard and omit my daily bath?'

Rosamund giggled feebly. 'I couldn't imagine you unkempt, which I fear I'm looking at this moment.'

'You've been working,' he excused her. 'But I know you're fastidious about your person. It's one of the things that pleases me about you.'

'You should know,' she murmured, thinking of the many times when, hot and sweaty from running, she had rushed to the shower. An imp of mischief showed in her amber eyes. 'What other things please you about me, or is that all?'

A shutter came down over his face and he turned away from her.

'Don't fish,' he said shortly.

'I know you've some regard for my athletic prowess,' Rosamund went on undeterred, 'or I shouldn't be here, but I'm not a mere running machine, Mr Belmont.'

'I never supposed you were,' he returned. 'It's the fact that you're not that frightens me.'

'Frightens you?' she echoed in astonishment.

'Women are so unpredictable.' He turned back to her and gave her a brilliant smile that made him look suddenly youthful. 'This is an unproductive conversation, so let's drop it. Since you won't be here tomorrow, I'll give you your Christmas present now. Come with me.'

He limped towards his study and Rosamund followed, protesting:

'Oh no! Mr Belmont, you've given me so much.'

He turned in the doorway, not denying it.

'But nothing personal. Christmas is the time for personal gifts, isn't it?' He went to his desk and took a flat package out of it. 'I thought this would match your eyes.'

That took her breath away. From the way he treated her, she would not have been surprised if he had never noticed the colour of her eyes. She took the package from him and held it, looking at it uncertainly.

'Well, aren't you going to open it?' he asked impatiently.

The case contained a necklace of yellow topaz set in gold.

'I . . . I can't take this,' she gasped. 'It's too valuable.'

'Not really, and it isn't new, it was my mother's. I had it cleaned, of course.' He put his head on one side, glancing down at the stones. 'I thought it looked like you.'

'But it's beautiful!'

'So are you ... sometimes.'

He said it so matter-of-factly that at first she did not grasp what he had said.

'You'll wear it at my party,' he went on; it was more a command than a question.

She was overwhelmed, stammering out her thanks, both by the present and the compliment. She had never possessed anything so lovely before.

'Put it on,' he bade her imperiously.

She hesitated and he took it from its case and himself fastened it about her neck. The dark wool of her sweater showed up the stones. Taking her by the arm, he led her to an oval mirror hanging over the fireplace. In it she saw her own reflection, her head no less bright than the necklace, her eyes almost the same tint. But she looked not at herself but at his dark face behind her. His blue eyes were glittering strangely, his well-shaped mouth compressed in a straight line, his nostrils slightly flared.

'It's perfect,' she said mechanically. His hands were clamped upon her shoulders and she was too much aware of him to give her mind to the trinket.

'Gold,' he murmured softly. 'Gold in your hair, your eyes and about your neck. My golden girl.'

A shiver of excitement ran down her spine. Was Adrian at last melting towards her? Her heartbeat quickened, he was so close and so dear, she could feel his breath on her neck. He went on:

'Next year, with luck, a still more precious gold will hang from your shoulders.'

Rosamund felt as if she had been douched with cold water. It pleased him to give her a necklace and she had for a moment dreamed she meant something to him as a woman, but all he thought of was that Olympic medal, which seemed to obsess him, and suppose she failed?

'We'll need all the luck there is,' she said with forced lightness. 'And now let me give you my little gift. I'll go and fetch it if you'll still be here.'

She ran back into the hall to retrieve her parcel from the pile beneath the tree, glad of the moment's respite to collect herself. What a fool she was to ever imagine she could be anything to Adrian!

He stared for a long time at the two bronze figures with a wry twist of his lips while Rosamund watched him anxiously.

'I . . . I didn't know what you'd like,' she faltered. 'This seemed appropriate.'

'Very,' his tone was dry. 'I was like that . . . once.'

'Oh!' Her hand flew to her mouth. She had never dreamed he would take it like that. 'I never thought.'

'Of course you didn't, and I'm glad you didn't,' he said quickly. 'It's a nice thing, Ros, full of life and movement. Thank you very much, I appreciate it.'

But Rosamund knew his first remark had expressed his real feelings and she had blundered. She was so used to his disability, and it was not conspicuous, that she forgot it often as not. But he never did and was abnormally sensitive about it. Being a man who admired physical perfection, he considered himself marred.

He put the statuette down on his desk. 'I shall keep it there,' he told her. 'It will bring back many pleasant memories.' He smiled at her downcast face. 'Don't look distressed, child. I like it immensely and it will serve as a reminder that . . .' He broke off with a grimace of pain.

'But I didn't want to remind you of . . . that,' she whispered.

'Of what? I didn't tell you. I'm quite used to my gammy knee, Ros, it's something I have to live with.'

He started to talk about their Christmas arrangements,

and told her he would drive her to her home after lunch.

'Please don't bother, there's a bus,' she began.

'It's no bother, and I'd like a word with your father. He'll be interested to hear of your progress. You mustn't waste your precious energy catching buses.'

Energy she needed for her running. Everything came back to that.

Returning to Belmont House two days later, Rosamund felt as if she were coming home, which was absurd because she was leaving her real home to come back to her place of business. Someone said home is where the heart is, and hers had become lodged at Belmont.

Her father was highly delighted by Adrian's continued interest in her career, but her mother, more discerning, sensed a change in her and suspected its cause. After their substantial Christmas dinner, to which Rosamund had done full justice—since she had gone into intensive training she was always unromantically hungry—Mrs Prescott asked suddenly:

'Don't you think you might do better if you went to a professional coach? We know Mr Belmont has been exceedingly generous both with his time and money, but you shouldn't impose upon him.'

'That's his look-out,' Paul Prescott interposed. 'He believes she's worth it and doesn't grudge either.'

Rosamund stared wide-eyed at her mother; how could she impose upon Adrian when he had from the first taken charge of her destiny, and resented any interference? Rather he had imposed upon her, restricting her independence. She said uncertainly:

'Mr Belmont would never agree to another coach. He has made a study of my special needs, no professional could devote so much interest to one particular athlete.'

'Exactly.' Doris Prescott gave her daughter a shrewd look.

'Don't go getting ideas,' Rosamund warned, her colour rising; she found she was unable to meet her mother's discerning eyes. 'He hopes I'm going to win a gold. That's all he thinks of.'

'And you? Is that all you think of?'

'Of course.'

Paul glanced from Rosamund's pensive face to his wife's anxious one.

'Now, Mother, don't you fret,' he admonished her. 'Ros is a sensible girl, and she knows that Mr Belmont is wholly interested in sport. When it comes to personal feelings, he would look a lot higher than our lass. He moves in a different circle and she knows it.' He chuckled throatily. 'From what I've heard, all the glamour girls are after him, because he's more than eligible, and when he does pick a wife, he'll look for style and elegance and perhaps a bit of money of her own.'

'I wasn't thinking of marriage,' Doris told him, while Rosamund writhed inwardly at her father's unintentional cruelty, or was he in his own way warning her too?

'Oh, he'd never get up to any hanky-panky,' Paul said confidently. 'I'm sure he's an honourable man and he knows Ros is innocent and unsophisticated—besides, I don't imagine he finds athletes very attractive in that way. He sees them at too great a disadvantage.'

'As nature made them?' Rosamund suggested with a forced laugh. 'No make-up and windblown hair, in vests and shorts.'

Mrs Prescott was not be diverted.

'But Ros might lose her heart, he's very good-looking.'

'Oh, there's no chance of that,' Rosamund declared emphatically. 'He's not my sort, too mature and cynical.

By the way, have you seen Tony lately?'

Her parents were diverted, as she had intended. They both liked Tony and Paul had seen him recently. Rosamund knew that she had lied about Adrian, but she did not want her mother to guess her secret. She had not shown them Adrian's gift to her or even told them that he had given her one. It might confirm their suspicions.

Adrian called for her as arranged with an excited Lucie in the car. The pantomime had been a huge success. He refused to come in, saying it would be long past Lucie's bedtime when they arrived home, and they must not delay. The Prescotts had sent small gifts for Lucie which Rosamund had hung on the tree. They came out to say hullo to the child, and Rosamund prompted her to thank them. Then she got into the back of the car beside her, and Lucie reverted to the pantomime as they sped through the December murk. The only blot on the performance of *Dick Whittington* was the wicked King Rat. He had come down into the stalls and Lucie would have been terrified if Uncle Adrian had not been beside her, but he was a match for a whole army of rats.

'I can contend with rats,' Adrian said from the front seat, 'but there are other monsters more formidable.'

'Like dragons?'

'You could call them dragons.'

'There wasn't none in the pantomime,' Lucie dismissed them, while Rosamund wondered to what Adrian referred. Abstract monsters, perhaps, like defeat and despair.

'You haven't thanked Ros for her present, have you?' Adrian reminded Lucie.

'Oh yes, thanks a lot, it was ever so nice, and Uncle Adrian gave me a pram to put it in.' Her small face became wistful. 'There was a lovely dolly on top of the tree, but Uncle Adrian said she was not for children to play with, and she was to be kept for next Christmas.'

'The unattainable always seems the more attractive,' Adrian remarked drily. 'The doll you've been given is a much better one, Lucie, you should be content with that.'

'It's very nice,' Lucie said dutifully, and sighed.

The unattainable, Rosamund thought, with her eyes on the dark head in front of her; was that the secret of his allure for her? Her parents had been emphasising unnecessarily that he was out of her reach, and it was foolish to hanker after what he could not give her, for like Lucie's fairy doll he was set far above her head and she must make do with something nearer to hand. That turned her thoughts towards Tony. She had not seen him for a long time, though they had exchanged cards at Christmas. Once she had thought her future lay with him, but he was not the man Adrian was and they had drifted apart, nor did she particularly wish to see him again. Adrian was lavish with his presents if he had given Lucie a doll's pram; he treated her almost as though she were his own child. Once she had wondered if she were, for she knew now that the child was illegitimate and that was why her mother's husband did not want her living with them, but had almost instantly rejected the supposition as a slur upon his character. Nor was there the slightest resemblance between round-faced, brown-eyed Lucie and Adrian's aquiline face and blue eyes. He was naturally benevolent, but his deeper feelings were not involved with any of them. Unconsciously she too sighed.

'Dear me, the back seat seems to be in the doldrums,' Adrian said mockingly. 'Cheer up, children, Christmas isn't over yet. There are still some good things in store.'

'Another present?' Lucie asked hopefully.

'No, you'll have to wait until your birthday for that,

though you may get a small gift from the vicar's wife when you go to her party on Saturday.'

'She won't give me a fairy doll,' Lucie said mournfully.

'We'll put a bit of tinsel and some wings on the one you've got,' Rosamund suggested.

Lucie shook her dark head. 'It wouldn't be the same.'

No, Rosamund agreed silently. Nothing could be the same as the object upon which one had set one's heart, and however she tried to dress Tony up in her thoughts he could never be a substitute for Adrian.

A young moon was a sickle in the clear sky as they sped up the lime tree avenue towards the house and hoar frost sprinkled the grass with silver. The house lights beckoned to them through the trees. This was home, but for how long?

Adrian drove to the side entrance and Lucie tumbled out of the car as soon as Rosamund opened the door and ran indoors, eager to tell her grandmother about the pantomime.

As she disappeared, Adrian said to Rosamund:

'We'll have to give her that doll when we dismantle the tree. I couldn't do so when the other children were here, but now it won't matter.'

'You couldn't be more indulgent if you were her real parent,' Rosamund told him.

He shot her a keen look. 'Do you imagine that I am?'

'Of course not!'

The light streaming out of the door Lucie had left open showed his impish grin, as they stood beside the car.

'You needn't pretend,' he went on, 'a lot of people do think so. Because I've tried to make a home for the poor little thing my actions have been misconstrued. There are a great many people in the world who can't credit a disinterested act of kindness.'

'I'm not one of them,' Rosamund said steadily. 'I've implicit faith in your integrity, Mr Belmont.'

Instantly he became mocking, as if he found her confidence naïve.

'What have I done to deserve such a tribute?' he demanded. 'I'm no saint, Ros, and if ever you meet Lucie's mother you'll know it's impossible that I could have had an affair with her. She's got a face like an amiable cow and a figure to match. However she got herself seduced is one of nature's mysteries. But it's cold out here, so run along indoors.'

He left her to drive the car into the garage and she went into the house.

Before she went to bed, Lucie dragged Rosamund into the hall to 'say goodnight' to the fairy doll. Preparations had already begun for the party next day. The dining room was to house a buffet meal, the drawing room would accommodate cards and sitting out, but the wide hall with its polished floor had been cleared for dancing. The tree still dominated the scene from its corner in all its glittering splendour. It would stay there until Twelfth Night. There had been an addition to the decorations since Rosamund had been away. Depending from the archway that led towards the drawing room a huge bunch of mistletoe had been hung.

Lucie pointed it out to her.

'Granny found we hadn't got any, so she asked the gardener to get her some. He found it growing on an apple tree.' The child's round brown eyes became rounder as she considered this extraordinary happening. 'It's a para ... para something.'

'Parasite? That's rather harsh. Some plants do grow on other plants, I don't think it hurts the apple tree.'

But did it sap its strength like ivy did? Rosamund

looked curiously at the pale green foliage and white berries. It grew on other trees beside apples, presumably also on oaks since it had been sacred in the time of the Druids, and had become traditional at Christmas.

'Granny says it's for kissing under,' Lucie informed her. 'Please kiss me.'

The rite was in progress when Adrian came down the stairs, the imposing carved staircase that Rosamund and Lucie never used, being related to the humbler back one. He was wearing a dark suit and looked every inch the lord of the manor as he made his descent.

'Ah, making use of Adela's importation,' he remarked.

Rosamund let Lucie slip to the floor, and she instantly ran to him, throwing her arms about his knees. 'Kiss me, Uncle Adrian.'

He swung her up.

'With pleasure, poppet.'

'Under the mistletoe,' she decreed, for they were some paces from it. He obligingly moved into position, with her chubby arms about his neck.

'Now Rosamund,' Lucie suggested as he put her down.

Adrian turned towards his protégée, his eyes glinting.

'Custom demands it,' he told her.

Rosamund backed away, her colour rising. She did not want casual salutes from Adrian Belmont; she knew his touch could inflame her, and was terrified that he might discover that it did.

'I don't think so, Mr Belmont,' she said demurely.

A wicked gleam came into his eyes.

'Afraid?'

'Of what should I be afraid, Mr Belmont?'

'Ah, what?' he mocked her. 'But since you're so reluctant, I'll excuse you ... this time. But as it's Christmas, couldn't you drop the Mr Belmont? My name, as you well know, is Adrian.'

'Uncle Adrian!' Lucie cried shrilly.

'Or if you prefer it, Uncle Adrian.'

'I'm not a child,' Rosamund said stiffly. The gap in years between them was not very great, they were the same generation, but there was a whole chasm of other things. 'I don't want to sound disrespectful. I believe most of your pupils call you Maestro.'

'Some of them do. So you want to keep me in my place?'

'No,' she returned dully. 'But I must remember mine.'

He seemed about to say something, but at that moment Mrs Grey came bustling in through the door that led to the back regions.

'Lucie, Lucie, come along, it's ever so late.'

'Granny, Uncle Adrian won't kiss Rosamund under the mistletoe,' Lucie informed her.

The housekeeper looked shocked. 'Of course not, most unsuitable,' she ejaculated. 'Come along, Lucie, bed.'

Lucie looked back to cry triumphantly, 'But he kissed me!'

Adrian laughed, gave Rosamund a wry look and went into his study. Disconsolately Rosamund followed Mrs Grey to her own place.

# CHAPTER FIVE

THE next day hummed with preparations for the party in the evening. Extra staff had been recruited from the village and food was being delivered by a local caterer. The gardener brought in baskets of wood to feed the log fires, for though the house was centrally heated, Adrian liked to augment it with open wood fires in the dining room and sitting room.

Lucie rushed from room to room in a wild state of excitement, getting in everyone's way, undamped by the fact that she would have gone to bed by the time the festivities began. Her grandmother had promised that she would set aside an assortment of goodies for her next day and if she was very good and not asleep, she would be allowed a glimpse of the dancing. Adrian had insisted that Adela should attend the party as a guest and the good woman, overwhelmed by such condescension, privately decided she would make herself useful by conducting the lady guests to the spare room that had been allocated as a powder room, and superintend the buffet when her employer was not looking.

Hothouse flowers also arrived from a florist in London to adorn the dining room tables and fill the handsome vases in the drawing room, but the wine was brought up from the Belmont cellars.

'Christmas comes but once a year,' the master of all this quoted tritely when Mrs Grey ventured to hint that he was being wildly extravagant. 'When I entertain I like to do the thing properly.'

85

Lavish to excess, Rosamund thought, viewing the preparations with a sinking heart. Adrian's small party seemed to have grown out of all proportion and she did not anticipate enjoying it. She feared he had invited someone special whom he wished to impress. Adela was always on the lookout for a possible new mistress. She considered it was high time Adrian selected a suitable bride, but Rosamund remembered he had said he was not a marrying man.

'You ought to have an heir, sir, to inherit Belmont,' Mrs Grey had said more than once, to which he had returned:

'You're being feudal, Adela, and in any case the tax man won't leave much to inherit.'

Though she expected to feel out of place among Adrian's guests, who would all be strangers to her, Rosamund was determined to look her best. She had in a moment of wild extravagance bought a yellow evening dress that had taken her fancy. Then it had seemed a piece of folly, but now she was glad she had it, for it was created for such an occasion. It had a close-fitting bodice, sleeveless and low-necked, from which the full chiffon skirt hung over a silk underskirt to her feet. It was of a deep amber colour and matched her eyes. Adrian's necklace enhanced it and gave it distinction. The gown might have been designed to show it off.

When the evening came, she bathed in scented bath salts, and brushed her hair until it shone. Now it fell in soft waves to her shoulders. She shadowed her eyes, so that they looked enormous, and applied colour to emphasise the soft curves of her mouth. She had no need of a blusher, for her cheeks were flushed with mingled dread and excitement. She knew she would not be a nonentity, her recent successes had ensured that, but she

would shrink from the critical eyes of Adrian's girl-
friends, recalling the supercilious glances of the couple
who way back in the summer had run with her and whom
she had beaten.

In sport as in the theatre a rising star met with more
jealousy than friendship, and her prowess would not
make her popular.

Her toilet completed, she surveyed herself critically in
the long glass fitted inside the wardrobe, and decided that
she would do Adrian credit, though he was unlikely to
admit it. She hungered to see admiration in his eyes.

The big stereogram downstairs was pouring out soft
music when she stepped out of her room into the long
corridor that led to the stairs. Tonight, being a guest, she
would use the main staircase, and she half hoped Adrian
would be there to see her come down it, for she knew it
would make an attractive setting for her dress. From
further down the passage she caught the sound of girlish
laughter from the open door of the spare room and their
scent perfumed the air. Most of them came from wealthy
homes in the neighbourhood, and some even boasted a
title, all eligible mates for the master of Belmont. Though
he kept Rosamund as secluded as a nun, Adrian was no
recluse himself, and tonight he was repaying all the
hospitality he had received.

Rosamund walked along the wide corridor thinking
of all the women of the past who had used it, holding up
their wide skirts from slippered feet. Women in lace and
silken furbelows, with powdered hair and patches on
their faces, coquettishly wielding their fans. They would
have been horrified at the idea of women athletes and
shocked by the scanty clothing of modern girls. Sport in
their day was confined to riding sidesaddle in sweeping
habits with plumed hats, and a little later to sedate games

of croquet. Even when tennis came in it had been played in long skirts and straw hats perched on curled pompadours. Much farther back in ancient Greece, the home of the Olympics, women did not take part in the games at all.

Thus musing, Rosamund came to the head of the carved staircase and looked down into the brightly lit hall. A crystal chandelier, not often used, depended from the ceiling, spilling light into every corner and dimming the illuminations on the Christmas tree.

Adrian was standing with a group of men underneath it. He was wearing a dinner jacket with a white carnation in his buttonhole, a pleated silk shirt and a black tie. The formal garb suited his dark good looks, fitting close to his slim waist and broad shoulders. His brown face was as usual immaculately shaved, his hair smooth as silk with the gloss of a raven's wing. He made the other men with him, most of whom were elderly, appear commonplace, even a little gross.

He looked up as if sensing Rosamund's approach and for a second held her gaze across the intervening distance. Her appearance was all that she had hoped, a charming picture, her pale dress standing out against the shadowed panelling behind her, her hair a red-gold glory about a neck and shoulders that seemed almost translucent. The gems about her throat glittered as they caught the light.

Seeing the direction of his eyes, the other men turned their heads to watch her descent, and a flicker of blue flame showed in his, but as she reached floor level, the shutter of indifference came down over his face, as he hastened to introduce her to his companions. Their expressions sharpened to interest, and they threw sly glances at their host. One of them said:

'We knew Belmont was harbouring a budding Atalanta,

but we didn't realise she was a beauty as well.'

'Atalanta's career was terminated by a gold apple,' Adrian returned suavely, 'but Rosamund is above such mundane temptations. She is dedicated, a vestal virgin serving the Olympic flame.'

He was well aware Rosamund's presence in his house was open to speculation, and sought by his veiled words to allay their conjectures. He might have been wiser to keep her in the background, but in actual fact he did not care what they thought.

Rosamund was recalling the legend of the Greek girl who was invincible until she stooped for the dropped apple, but her conqueror rewarded her with his love. Alas, if she lost her races there would be no loving arms to console her, only bitter words. As for her position at Belmont, these were permissive days and she was no more concerned with the possible ambiguity of her situation than Adrian was. Actually it did not occur to her that it might be open to criticism.

Adrian ushered her into the sitting room and made her known to the older women assembled there. Their names did not register with her, there were too many of them, though some she recognised as being well known in sporting circles; the young people he did not present, knowing they dispensed with such ceremony. Rosamund became aware of covert assessing glances. She was Adrian Belmont's new find, but was she a potential champion or merely a flash in the pan?

An elderly man asked her to dance and she circled the floor with him in a slow waltz.

'I'm no good at modern gymnastics,' he told her. 'This is about all I can manage nowadays.'

Some of the young people were looking bored, awaiting a change in the music.

'Belmont is expecting great things of you,' her partner told Rosamund, as if she did not know that only too well. 'We're looking forward to next season when we'll know if you can fulfil your promise.'

She realised she was dancing with one of the selectors.

'I only hope I can,' she said fervently.

'If you run as well as you dance,' he said gallantly, 'you will.'

And then looking at the people lining the wall she saw Tony Bridges. Tony, elegant in a dinner suit, still bronzed by a fiercer sun than that of England and looking slightly bored with the fair-haired girl who was talking to him. His eyes met hers and his face brightened. He was waiting for her when her partner relinquished her.

'Ros darling, how lovely you look!' he exclaimed as he came up to her. 'Why do we never see you around these days?'

'I was running at the White City not so long ago,' she pointed out.

'But you vanished before I could get near you. You won your events, I seem to remember. Is it true that old Adrian keeps you locked in an ivory tower and won't give the press men entry, still less your old friends?'

'I haven't got any except you, Tony, and you've been away. I'm working very hard and have no time for socialising.'

'Yes, I know Belmont's methods,' he said with a grimace. 'But you mustn't let him monopolise you. After all, you do the running, not he, and you've a right to a bit of fun.'

'Fun and athletics don't team well.'

'Don't you believe it. I went out with a Commonwealth team to Los Angeles, and boy, did we hit the wire!'

'Did you do well?' she asked.

'Middling,' he admitted, and she surmised that the social life had spoilt his form. She led him on to speak of his achievements, which had not been spectacular. He had not won anything, though he had come second once or twice.

'I doubt I'll qualify for the Olympic team,' he told her gloomily.

'You might if you worked harder,' Rosamund suggested.

He shrugged his shoulders. 'Too much of a drag. There are other things in life besides medals.'

They stayed together for the rest of the evening. Tony, like herself, did not know many people there. He had, he told her, run into Adrian previously at a London club and had been given a casual invitation.

'Thought I'd like to see the place again, and I heard rumours that you were still here.'

'I've got a job here,' she told him.

'Oh, is that still on?' He grinned mischievously. 'Shouldn't you be baby-sitting?'

'This is my night off.'

Soon they were on the old easy intimate footing.

'I was afraid you'd forgotten me,' Rosamund told him.

'Well, darling, you know how it is with athletics, they are demanding,' he explained. 'But now we've met again we must keep in closer touch.' There was a sensual gleam in his eyes as he looked at her.

Rosamund agreed, but halfheartedly, for she no longer fancied herself in love with Tony and wondered if it was fair to encourage him. She had been thankful to find him there among a crowd of not very friendly strangers, but she had changed since she had been his girl and sooner or later she must tell him so. Then it occurred to her that he had probably amused himself with plenty of counter-attractions since last they had met and she had no reason to suppose he was serious about her. It would be very pleasant to have a friend of her own age again, but without strings attached.

They danced and Tony introduced her to some of the latest steps, twisting and twirling to the exciting rhythms the stereogram was now playing. The older people had retired to play cards in the drawing room and there was no sign of Adrian. Rosamund was subconsciously watching for a glimpse of his elegant figure, not knowing that he had retired with some of his sporting cronies to his study.

Exhausted by their strenuous dancing, they went to help themselves from the delicious dishes spread out on the buffet, where Adela presided in defiance of Adrian's orders, attired in black silk with an Irish lace bertha. She smiled at Rosamund.

'I allowed Lucie to have a look at the dancing,' she confided to her. 'Luckily she was too sleepy to want to join in. She said you looked like a fairy yourself.'

'Discerning child,' Tony laughed when Rosamund had explained who Lucie was. 'Ros dances like a fairy, though she's not exactly gossamer. Couldn't run if she was.'

Adela looked doubtfully at Tony, recognising him as the young man who had been responsible for Rosamund's coming to Belmont. Her expression became slightly disapproving, and Rosamund guessed she feared the good-looking Tony Bridges might seek to disrupt her training. How wrong she was; Tony could not tempt her from Adrian.

'It's very hot,' he said when they had eaten all they required. 'Would it be asking too much of you to come outside? I want to get some cool, and see the place where I used to lodge.'

Rosamund agreed and went to fetch her coat. Together they stole out of the side door into the quiet night. It was frosty and still, the stars very bright.

'Has Belmont any young hopefuls here now?' Tony asked as they approached the training complex.

'No, he doesn't seem interested in anyone but me,' Rosamund told him, and blushed in the darkness as he whistled. 'It's quite impersonal,' she went on hastily. 'He's got an obsession about training a gold medallist and he seems to think I can qualify.'

'Don't you find such concentration too much of a good thing?' Tony suggested. 'After all, we're only young once and these are the best years of your life. Do you want to be sacrificed on the altar of Adrian Belmont's ambition?'

'I don't know what you mean,' she hedged, though she had an idea. 'He can't make me do anything I don't want to do.'

'Don't be too sure of that. The fellow has an almost hypnotic power when he wants something. It was quite a relief to get out of his clutches.'

Rosamund suspected that Adrian had lost interest in Tony because he considered he was too frivolous to make the grade. Not wanting to discuss her employer further with him, she changed the subject.

The buildings were locked, but through the windows they could discern dimly the objects in the gymnasium by the light of the torch Tony produced from the pocket of his duffle coat. Flashing it in at the hostel windows, he identified the bunk he had occupied.

'Wasn't too bad living here,' he told her. 'I was starry-eyed in those days and dreamed of standing on an

Olympic rostrum. Rather disillusioned nowadays, Ros. The selectors are so unpredictable. They don't always choose the best.' This she guessed was his excuse for his mediocre performances. 'Besides, the black men have such an advantage,' he continued to grumble. 'They're born and bred to it, and we of the decadent West haven't a chance against them when it comes to running.'

'Nevertheless I hope to hold my own against any colour of girl,' she was provoked into saying.

'I hope you do, Ros, but is running all you think about?' He slid his arm about her waist. 'At one time you were more interested in having a home and family.'

They were walking back towards the house from which departing guests were emerging, as it was getting very late.

'Plenty of time for that when I've won my laurels,' she said lightly. There had been a time when Tony's intentions had been of importance to her, but now she was anxious to avoid any sentiment on his part, since her fancy for him had died. She regretted it was so, because he might have been able to cure her of her hopeless infatuation with Adrian. With that thought in mind, she decided to make an attempt to blow upon the ashes of her feeling for him in the hope that if she could rekindle them they might obliterate the later flame.

When they re-entered the hall they found it deserted; the guests had gone and most of the lights had been turned out including the chandelier, but the Christmas tree still shone in its corner, a reminder of festivities now on the wane.

'I suppose I must be off,' Tony said, regretfully, for it was warm and intimate in the dim hall. 'Where's Belmont? I must say goodbye.'

'I expect he's in the other room, I'll fetch him.' Rosamund slipped off her coat, dropping it on to a chair, and went towards the connecting archway. Tony, following her, stopped her beneath the mistletoe.

'Come, give me a kiss under the mistletoe, that's expected of you,' he said, laughing, and took her in his arms.

Rosamund submitted to his embrace and the kisses he rained upon her face, striving with all her might to raise an answering ardour, but it was no use. Tony's one-time appeal for her was entirely dead and his caresses repelled her.

'What's the matter with you?' he asked, raising his face from hers. 'You never used to be frigid.'

'My salad days,' she quoted sadly. 'Oh, Tony, everything has changed.'

Disappointed, he said acidly: 'So it seems, or else I've lost my touch. Let's try again.' He bent his head, but a sharp voice cracked behind them.

'It's very late, Bridges, and most of the guests have gone.'

Adrian had come out of the card room and though it was too dim to see his expression, Rosamund sensed he was furious. Because Tony had outstayed the other guests, or because he was kissing her? Neither fault seemed to call for anger on his part.

Tony hastily disengaged himself from her and addressed his host.

'Sorry, sir, I didn't mean to outstay my welcome,' he said stiffly, 'but we'd been outside and I forgot the time.'

'Outside, in the cold?'

'Tony wanted to sentimentalise over the complex,' Rosamund explained. 'I wasn't cold, I had my coat.'

They had moved back into the hall, and Adrian switched on more light. His glance flickered over Rosa-

mund, noting her disarranged hair. But he spoke more
genially.

'You can stay as long as you like, Tony, it's Ros I'm
concerned about. She's in strict training and she should
be in bed. I thought she was.'

Rosamund saw he was very pale and his eyes were
glittering like blue ice.

'It's Christmas,' she protested feebly.

'All the same, late hours are bad for you. You'd better
go up at once.'

His peremptory tone stung her. 'I'm not Lucie to be
ordered to bed,' she declared defiantly. 'And I haven't
seen Tony for ages. I shall stay up just as long as I
like!'

'May I remind you, Miss Prescott, that you're working
in my house and I expect my employees to obey my
orders.'

Rosamund's face whitened. As a rule he never referred to her position and to do so in front of her friend
was intentionally humiliating, but before she could think
of a retort, Tony intervened.

'It's no good, Ros, I know him of old. If he says bedtime, bedtime it is. You'd better obey the martinet.' He
glanced at his watch. 'My God, it is late. My fault, sir,
we were so absorbed in our mutual reminiscences time
just flew. Goodnight, Ros, be seeing you. Goodnight,
sir, thanks for the splendid evening.'

He held out his hand and Adrian shook it perfunc-
torily. He walked with Tony to the door, which he bolted
and locked behind him.

Rosamund stood where he had left her, trying to control her temper. Tony's words came back to her. Adrian
might have hypnotic powers, but she was not his doormat, nor was she a sacrifice upon his altar.

'Am I a martinet?' he asked gently.

'Definitely,' she told him, but already she was relenting as she noticed his face looked strained. He had had a very exhausting day.

'It's the only way to get results,' he excused himself. His eyes glinted. 'I dislike necking on my premises, it's vulgar.'

'Then why did you put up the mistletoe?'

'I didn't, it was Adela's idea.'

He limped past her and stretching upward, tore the bunch down. There was such restrained passion in his action that Rosamund stared at him in astonishment.

'Was it necessary to do that?' she asked. 'It looked so pretty.'

'A relic of superstition,' he almost snarled. 'An encouragement to loose manners.'

'It's part of the season's ritual.' Rosamund supposed he was venting his ill humour on the harmless plant instead of herself, but she could not understand how she had sinned, unless he was afraid Tony had been trying to undermine his influence.

She fetched her coat, but Adrian stood between her and the stairs, the mistletoe, its white berries scattering, on the ground by his feet. She picked it up, looking at him reproachfully, and put it on a chair.

'A shame to let it be trampled upon.'

'You're strangely sentimental about a bunch of greenery,' he said harshly, 'but it served your purpose.'

'A friendly kiss underneath it?'

'Is that what you call it? I'd describe it as a passionate embrace.'

'I don't see how you could assess it in the dark, and after all, is it your business, Mr Belmont? Aren't you being rather unreasonable?'

His face cleared and he smiled sadly.

'Forgive me, Ros, I'm acting like Scrooge, but what else can you expect from a cripple with a warped mind?'

'Oh, Adrian!' She took an impulsive step towards him, shocked by his description of himself. 'You're not a cripple. Why, I never remember that you're ... a little lame.'

'But I never forget it.' His intent blue gaze wandered hungrily over her white shoulders, her slenderness emphasised by the long dress, the glory of her hair and her pale face in which her amber eyes were big with compassion, an emotion he hated to see expressed.

'I used to dance once,' he went on savagely, 'but I never shall again. Your friend is an expert performer in more ways than one. I don't blame you for enjoying his company. Does he kiss as well as he dances?'

Rosamund wilted under the sudden blaze in his eyes, his bitter tone.

'Oh, Adrian!' she protested.

'Oh, Adrian,' he mimicked her, mocking her. 'Go to bed.'

'Not yet.' Her courage returned in a sudden flood, she could not bear to leave him like this. His strange behaviour would indicate jealousy—oh, not of her affections, she would not presume to imagine that, but of Tony's youth and unmaimed body. She wanted to assure him that to her they just were not comparable.

'Please, Mr Belmont, I'd like you to know that Tony doesn't mean anything to me. I proved that tonight.'

'Why should you think that such a discovery is of any interest to me?' he asked coldly.

'Because ... because ...' she faltered, then added firmly, 'I felt you might imagine he was distracting me from you.'

'From me?' His mouth twisted sardonically. 'My dear little girl, please don't transfer your youthful heart from him to me. All I want from you is that gold medal. When you've won it, our ways will part.'

'Then I hope I never win it,' she cried recklessly.

'You dare say that!' He came towards her, gripping both her wrists, hurting her. 'You little idiot, would you waste all my time and endeavour, all your time and effort to support a schoolgirl crush—because that, I suppose, is at the bottom of your foolishness. You're just like all your sex, swayed by emotional involvement. If you want that, by God you shall have it. I can kiss better than Master straight-legged Bridges, even if I have got a crooked knee. I'll even take you to bed, if that'll satisfy you, but you're going to win that medal!'

He pulled her roughly towards him and shifted his grip to enfold her in his arms. It was not like the night in the moonlight, but a fierce punishing onslaught that crushed her body ruthlessly against him and ravished her mouth. Nor did Rosamund respond as she had done upon that previous occasion. She was numb with shock and horror at what he had said, the low opinion he had of her.

The storm passed and he released her abruptly, passing his hand wearily across his brow.

'That,' Rosamund whispered through bruised lips, 'was unforgivable.'

'So was what you said,' he flashed. 'For God's sake don't ever so provoke me again.'

'I won't, because I shan't be here.'

'You'll stay,' his jaw set determinedly, 'if I have to lock you in your room.'

'The tyrant act won't work with me,' she retorted. 'I'll not be bullied!'

His face changed, the harshness smoothed away and he said gently:

'Poor little Ros, what an ill-mannered cur I am! But you won't leave me, for I've done a lot for you and you wouldn't be so ungrateful. You see, I know your character, my dear, and you couldn't let me down.'

She lifted her head proudly. 'You're right, Mr Belmont, I won't do that, I'll win that gold for you if it kills me. But don't you ever dare to touch me again.'

She picked up her coat which had fallen to the floor and trailed up the stairs submerged in a wave of hatred for Adrian Belmont. She had never hated anyone before, but there was no mistaking the black bitter tide that welled up at her at the thought of his arrogance. He was a cruel beast, a despot, and heartless, with no scruples as to what means he used to get his own way.

She was unaware that he followed her to the foot of the staircase and watched her ascent with a curiously wistful expression, his mocking mouth softened to tenderness. He went back into his own room and drew the figurine of the two runners towards him. His long sensitive fingers probed the smooth metal, lingering over the knee joints. Then with a sigh, he carried it to a cupboard in the wall and thrust it into its darkest depths.

Meanwhile, Rosamund was unclasping the topaz necklace from her throat. She decided that she must return it to Adrian. She could not accept such a present from a man she loathed to the depths of her being—or so she assured herself she did. That evening he had humiliated her in every possible way. Yet her fingers lingered over the jewels as she put it back in its case. It had belonged to his mother, he had told her. What sort of a woman had Mrs Belmont been, and had she loved her little son before she went to her premature death? Were the grandparents who replaced her kind to him? Was it her loss that had made Adrian the granite man he had become? Adela Grey had told her that he had thrown himself into athletics with a passion that suggested some unfulfilled need in his life until his accident denied him that solace. A warped mind, he had said; perhaps his trouble was he had lost the capacity to love. His attitude towards most human beings was a cynical detachment, while he did not hesitate to play upon their weaknesses to gain his own ends. Only towards Lucie and in his respect for Mrs Grey did he show any humanity. She must learn to be hard and unemotional too, a running robot, impervious even to hate.

She shut the case on the yellow stones and pushed it deep down into a drawer to await a suitable opportunity to return it. She did not want to provoke another scene with Adrian just yet, though surely he would understand that she could not keep it after what had occurred. But when had he ever understood her feelings? He would much prefer that she did not have any, and tonight he had cruelly misjudged her. She had been a fool to so betray herself; he did not want pity from her and resented any hint of affection. From henceforth she must keep herself coolly aloof until she had done what he wanted her to do, for as he had said, she could not be so ungrateful as to desert him.

She undressed and got into bed, but when the soothing darkness enveloped her, hate, wounded pride and her sense of bitter rejection were washed away in a storm of passionate weeping.

# CHAPTER SIX

JANUARY that year was mild but not very pleasant, with grey skies and chilly winds. Rosamund felt dull and flat without the excitement of racing. There were indoor events, but Adrian scorned them, nor after one experience did Rosamund want another. The boards, the banked-up track and dazzling lights required a different technique and she found them restricting and confusing. She won her event, competition was not strong, but did not break any record. As a diversion Adrian sent her out on cross-country runs with the local harrier club, which she disliked even more. The other girls were either too inquisitive or malicious. They were curious about her relationship with the Master of Belmont or jealous of her successes. She outclassed them and usually came in well ahead of the rest of the field, which did not endear her to them. The heavy going, often in drizzle or mist, had none of the exhilaration engendered by a swift quarter mile on a hard track.

Since the night of the party, she and Adrian had accepted a kind of truce. At their first encounter on the following day, Rosamund felt embarrassed and a little shamefaced, for she had triggered him off by a foolish and unnecessary statement, but if he apologised she was ready to forgive him. He did nothing of the sort; apologies were not Adrian Belmont's line. He merely suggested that they had indulged too freely in party spirit, and the incident could be forgotten. Offended by his casual manner, Rosamund agreed with hauteur, but she did not

102

forgive him. The implication that he had been tipsy was
no excuse, especially as she was quite certain he had been
perfectly sober. She avoided his company as much as
possible and treated him with cool disdain, but he was
not affected by her displeasure, giving her quizzical looks
and addressing her with exaggerated courtesy which only
inflamed her all the more.

A more pleasant addition to her activities was the red
Mini. Lucie had started school, but the village school
was a mile away, and the walk an ordeal in bad weather.
Adrian decided she should be taken by car, and Rosamund must learn to drive his second car, the Mini he kept
for such errands. He proceeded to teach her himself, and
she surprised both him and herself by displaying a natural aptitude at the wheel, in a very short time acquiring
complete control of the little car. After a study of the
Highway Code, she passed her test without putting a
hand or foot wrong. The examiner could not believe that
she had not been driving for years. Rosamund wondered
if this was another example of the hypnotism which
Tony had declared Adrian possessed. But whatever had
inspired her, the results were very satisfactory, for now
she was mobile. She even chauffeured for Adrian upon
occasion when he wanted to be taken somewhere and
collected at a later time. She was glad of that, because
she felt she was doing more to earn her salary. Now she
could visit other tracks at the weekends, her preference
being the one at the Crystal Palace where the stadium
manager was friendly to her and she met other runners.
One afternoon after a practice run with several other
girls, a man came up to her and introduced himself as the
British team coach, who she knew had trained the last
Olympic team and would probably perform the same
service for the next.

'You're one of Belmont's runners?' he asked, and she confirmed that she was.

'He's an eye for talent and knows how to bring it out. He ought to have my job, but he won't accept an official post. He never concerns himself except with championship potential and I've never known him to be interested in a girl before. He must consider you quite exceptional.'

Rosamund blushed. 'That remains to be seen.'

'You're fleet as a deer. Of course you lack experience, but outsiders have won championships before today. We'll be watching you.'

Elated, Rosamund drove home dreaming of future victories, and encountered Adrian as she came out of the garage.

'The Crystal Palace seems to agree with you,' he remarked, misinterpreting her radiant expression, 'better than Belmont.'

'I go there to get some competitive running,' she explained, meeting his eyes with a challenge in hers. 'And to find some pleasant company.'

'Tony Bridges, of course?'

'He wasn't there.'

'Your looks belie you. Don't try to deceive me, Miss Prescott. You're welcome to meet whom you choose, so long as you don't neglect your training.'

Rosamund had meant to tell him what the coach had said to her, but Adrian's suspicions checked her. His eyelids flickered under her wide indignant stare, and he turned his head away.

'You can't blame me for seeking company elsewhere,' she observed, 'since you don't give me much of yours.'

His eyes flashed back to hers with a glint in their blue depths.

'Have you missed me?'

'More than I wanted you. I couldn't fail to miss your caustic comments.'

'I was never one to deal in sugar plums,' he retorted. 'If you're collecting them at the stadium, let me assure you my caustic comments are far more beneficial.'

With which barbed speech, he limped away from her towards the house.

Then, later in the year, the Delaneys came to stay, a mother and daughter who lived in the French Haute Savoie. Dr Delaney was an eminent French doctor; he was unable to get away, but his wife had been ailing and it was thought that a change would do her good. Adrian had met the family when he had toured the continent before his accident on a series of international fixtures. The doctor took a keen interest in athletics and admired the brilliant young competitor. He invited Adrian to spend a winter holiday with them, promising him good skiing. Madeleine, his daughter, was as expert on the pistes as Adrian was on the track and had competed in winter sports events. Thus they had a common bond, even though their fields of action were different.

It was Adela Grey who told Rosamund about the Delaneys, and Rosamund discovered the housekeeper was viewing the coming visit with great satisfaction, for she had convinced herself there was more than friendship between her employer and his guest. In the cosy atmosphere of her sitting room, with Lucie safe in bed, she became expansive.

'He's always taken girls out,' she told Rosamund, 'but he's never serious about any of them, it's never the same one for more than a week or so.' Then catching the critical look in Rosamund's eyes, she hastened to defend him. 'I don't blame him, he's still a young man and the hussies do run after him. Why shouldn't he take what they offer? But Miss Delaney's different, he respects her, and she's old enough to have some sense. Twenty-eight to his twenty-nine.' Rosamund was surprised, she had thought Adrian was much older, but his accident had left its mark upon him.

'Has she been here before?' she asked.

'Once, about four years ago, when he was still a whole man. My goodness, what an energetic couple they were! She rode every day, hunted when there was a meet and danced every night, either having a party here or he took her up to London. He was in training, of course, and he said she played havoc with his schedule, but it was winter time so it didn't matter too much. I thought he'd pop the question before she left, but it was Olympics year and he said he wanted to win his gold first. Then that summer ... poor Mr Adrian ... it wasn't even his fault, the car that ran into him was on the wrong side of the road and the driver was drunk.'

The housekeeper paused and wiped her eyes. Even at this distance of time, the recollection of the accident moved her.

'But didn't Mademoiselle Delaney come to him?' Rosamund asked, for in similar circumstances she would have rushed to console her man.

'No.' Mrs Grey compressed her lips. 'I think he told her not to. Oh, he was in a sorry state—he fired me more than once, but I refused to budge. I'd served his grandfather and father before him, nice gentlemen they were too. Both died before their time, the old one with a coronary; so I wouldn't leave Belmont even though Mr Adrian snapped my head off.'

Rosamund was still thinking about Madeleine Delaney. 'I'd have come just the same,' she insisted.

'Yes, Miss Rosamund.' Adela's eyes twinkled. 'We

know even high walls with spikes on 'em couldn't keep
you out. Lucky fellow your young man.'

About to tell her Tony was not her young man, Rosamund checked herself. She did not want Mrs Grey to
suspect the direction in which her heart was turning. She
was still resentful of Adrian's treatment of her, but her
burning hate had subsided, she rather feared it had been
another facet of her love, the reverse of the coin, and
Adela's story was arousing all her sympathies.

'The Master doesn't want pity,' the housekeeper went
on. 'He'd think that was motivating her, and no doubt
he'd snubbed her. He's a very proud man.'

'Too much so,' Rosamund exclaimed. 'Pride can create
such a barrier.'

Wasn't it her own pride that had come between herself
and Adrian? Because he had reacted violently to her
provocation on the night of the party, she had hidden
behind a barrier of icy reserve. He had wanted to forget
the incident, but she could not forgive it. Not that he
cared about her feelings, she had only deprived herself.
Now, with the coming of this old flame of his, there was
no possibility of resuming their former friendly attitude.
He might even lose interest in her running.

Mrs Grey went on: 'But all that's in the past. Now
she's coming again they'll take it up from where they
started—or so I hope. At least she hasn't taken up with
anyone else. He needs a wife, Miss Rosamund, and Belmont should have a mistress; it should have an heir. He
broods too much, a family would take him out of himself.'

'I daresay.' Rosamund found the conversation was becoming painful. In her opinion Madeleine Delaney had
failed Adrian in his darkest hour, but knowing how
prickly he could be, perhaps she was not entirely to

blame. A young, sensitive girl could be easily rebuffed if she felt her love was being rejected.

The Delaneys arrived one wet cold evening. Rosamund had fetched Lucie from school and as she stopped the Mini at the side door, she saw Adrian's big car coming up the drive. Impelled by a strong curiosity to see the girl Adela was sure Adrian intended to marry, she bade Lucie run indoors out of the wet, while she put the car away, and as soon as the child had gone, moved stealthily round the side of the house. Standing screened by a laurel bush, she watched the visitors decant from the car. Adrian was helping the older woman to get out of the back seat, while Madeleine Delaney collected bags and wraps. Rosamund saw her clearly as she turned towards the house—a tall young woman, who was almost incredibly thin in a smart tailor-made suit with a handsome fur jacket slung across her shoulders. She wore a small felt hat which hid her hair and her sharp-featured face was skilfully made up. The overall impression she gave was of stylish sophistication, she showed off her clothes like a mannequin, and her gait and figure would have graced such a calling. She had all a Frenchwoman's chic.

Rosamund was conscious of a feeling of repulsion, for though she was not near enough to see much detail Madeleine Delaney gave her the impression of being as hard as nails. She understood now why she had not come to Adrian in his hour of need.

They'll suit each other, she thought, bitterly; his heart's atrophied and she hasn't got one.

Lucie too was curious and, fearful that she might stray, both Rosamund and her grandmother tried to impress upon her that when Uncle Adrian had visitors she must keep in her own part of the house. Downstairs this was not difficult, for the back quarters were divided from the front by a single fireproof door which was too heavy for her to open; upstairs the accommodation was intermingled. Lucie had become the proud possessor of the fairy doll, though the toy was soon spoiled, for in common with so many little girls Lucie had an urge to undress her dolls. The tinsel clothing was not meant for such treatment and more often than not the poor fairy lay naked, despoiled of her finery. Rosamund's present was more practical, her garments could be taken off and her wardrobe had been augmented with small hand-knitted articles made by Lucie's grandmother; her complexion, though, had suffered by repeated washing.

When Rosamund took Lucie upstairs that night to go to bed, the child gave her the slip while she was running her bath.

The guests' bedrooms were situated in the front of the house, Rosamund's room and the bathroom were at the end of the passage, overlooking the side of the premises, Lucie and Mrs Grey's were at the back. Coming into the corridor, Rosamund heard voices from Madeleine's room. The door was slightly ajar, and Lucie's clear treble indicated that she had found her quarry.

'Can I put some of that stuff on my face?'

Rosamund tapped on the door. 'Lucie,' she called, 'your bath's ready.'

'Oh, bother!' exclaimed Miss Lucie.

'Run along, your *bonne* waits for you.' Madeleine's voice was high-pitched and unmusical. 'You do not need the rouge with your cheeks like apples. *Bonne nuit, mon enfant.*'

Lucie came reluctantly. Rosamund caught a glimpse of Madeleine's tall figure in a quilted wrap and an array of pots and jars on the glass topped dressing table. Evidently Mademoiselle Delaney was unpacking.

'Naughty girl!' she scolded Lucie. 'You mustn't go in there.'

'The door wasn't prop'ly shut and I only peeped,' Lucie explained. 'The lady *asked* me to come in. She's got stuff to make white cheeks pink.'

'As she said, you don't need any,' Rosamund told her.

In bed with the washed-out doll beside her, Lucie remarked pensively: 'My dolly's gone all pale.'

'You scrubbed her too hard. Goodnight, darling.'

Rosamund kissed the child, lit the nightlight she always left with Lucie and went downstairs. Adela would snatch a moment in the midst of her preparations for dinner to say goodnight to her granddaughter. Ellen, the only staff who slept in at Belmont, was helping with the preparations and a village woman had come in to wash up. She and Ellen would eat in the kitchen when dinner was over while Rosamund and Adela had theirs on trays in the housekeeper's room.

Mrs Grey was disgruntled when Ellen brought the dishes out of the dining room. Madeleine Delaney was on a diet and had refused the choice confections she had prepared in her honour, asking for salad which had not been provided, an apple and cheese.

'A lot of fiddle-faddle,' she snorted. 'Diet my foot! She's nothing but a bag of bones. She'd look better with a bit of meat on her.'

Ellen, a stout country girl, giggled.

'Men like curves,' she declared smugly, stroking her own fine bust. 'They don't want to sleep with a skeleton.'

'Don't be coarse,' Adela snapped. 'They don't fancy bolsters either.' She looked pointedly at Ellen's avoirdupois.

'That's where you're wrong, Mrs Grey. My boy-friend likes cushiony women.'

'Then he's got one. Come along, Miss Rosamund,'—
Rosamund had objected to the formality of Miss Prescott,
but could not persuade the housekeeper to drop the Miss
—'supper's ready and at least you never turn up your
nose at my cooking.'

Mrs Grey had her own small television set which provided their evening's entertainment. They sat on either
side of the fire, Rosamund's mind absent from the programme she was supposed to be watching. How was
Adrian entertaining his guests? Were they viewing too?
Would he come down to the track in the morning? Mrs
Grey was knitting placidly and the house was very quiet.
When a muffled cry reached them from upstairs, Rosamund and Adela looked at each other, then, impelled by
the same thought, raced for the back stairs. Outdistan-
cing the older woman, Rosamund reached Lucie's room
far ahead of her. The door was open and it was empty,
but sounds came from Mademoiselle Delaney's, which
door was also open. Rosamund stopped on the threshold
as Adela came puffing up to her. Inside was a scene of
chaos. The stool in front of the dressing table had been
overturned, a handsome sheepskin rug was rumpled up
as if someone had fallen over it, and all the little pots and
jars on the dressing table were either overturned or
strewn over the carpet. Lucie's doll, her face bedaubed
with rouge and eye-shadow, lay on the bed, and Lucie
herself was screaming, her hands over a red mark on her
face caused by a vicious slap. The lady guest, seething
with anger, towered over her.

As she saw her grandmother, Lucie's shrieks changed
to loud sobs.

'She . . . hit me!' she gasped.

'*Vilaine, méchante enfant!*' Madeleine shouted. She
picked up a jar from the floor. 'My costly *feuilles des*

*roses*!' She advanced on the child again, but in one swift movement Rosamund caught her wrist. At close quarters she could see the French girl's face, which was narrow and high-bred, with small dark eyes under well cared-for arched eyebrows. At that moment it was distorted with rage.

'Please, Mademoiselle Delaney, do calm down,' Rosamund besought her. 'Lucie has been very naughty, but you shouldn't hit her.'

'Do not touch me, *paysanne*!' With surprising strength Madeleine twisted her wrist free and aimed another blow at the unfortunate Lucie, catching her on the side of her head, her rings breaking the skin. Lucie yelled, Mrs Grey started forward uttering protests, while Rosamund said something much stronger than protests as she placed herself between the infuriated woman and the child.

'What's going on here?' Adrian's quiet voice reached them from the doorway and the uproar died away. He was immaculate in evening clothes and his keen glance rested on each of them in turn, taking in every detail of the scene.

Madeleine rushed to him, throwing herself into his arms, pouring out a torrent of French, while Adela gathered the near-hysterical Lucie into her embrace, wiping away the few drops of blood that oozed from her temple with one of Madeleine's tissues. Rosamund picked up the stool and put it in its place.

'*Tais-toi!*' Adrian disengaged himself from Madeleine's clinging arms. She was almost as tall as he was, and her slinky black gown empasised her height and slenderness. With his hand at her waist, he looked sternly at Rosamund.

'Miss Prescott, will you explain what you are doing in Mademoiselle Delaney's room?'

Lucie lifted a tear-stained face from Adela's shoulder.

'Dolly too pale ... lady got pink stuff ...' she hiccupped. 'She hit me.'

As he realised what had happened, Adrian's mobile mouth twitched, and he glanced at the doll's rainbow complexion.

Madeleine cried shrilly: 'She should be beaten!'

'No, Madeau,' he told her gently. 'We don't beat children at Belmont, but she shall be suitably punished.'

'She's been punished enough,' Rosamund declared hotly. 'Look at her face!'

Madeleine stared malignantly at Rosamund, her dark eyes narrowed to slits. She appraised her red-gold hair, her flushed face which anger made beautiful—too good-looking to be an inmate of Adrian Belmont's house.

'Ah, yes, the *bonne*,' she said nastily. 'Adrian, do you permit her to speak to you? She neglects her duties, she permits the child to roam free without supervision. Only this afternoon she was again in my room, pestering me. You are too easy-going, *mon ami*, allowing these people to impose upon you. Dismiss the maid at once!'

'I will deal with her in my own way,' Adrian told her smoothly. He looked across at Rosamund and his glance was like blue steel. 'It seems you've been negligent, Miss Prescott, allowing Lucie to escape from your control. Also I cannot permit my servants to be impertinent to my guests. Didn't Mrs Grey make it clear to you that Lucie was to stay in her own part of the house? I consider you're to blame for ... all this.' He indicated the room with a sweeping gesture. 'I suppose you were too engrossed in ... er ... television to keep an eye on your charge.' He turned his gaze to the black willow wand within the circle of his arm. 'I'm sorry this has happened, Madeau, but you shan't be disturbed again.'

'I would feel more sure of that if you found a more competent nursemaid,' Madeleine persisted.

'Unfortunately Miss Prescott would be difficult to replace,' Adrian stated enigmatically. He winked at Rosamund, but she was too incensed to notice. A tide of furious indignation swamped her. He knew as well as anybody that it was impossible to keep Lucie under constant surveillance, and he often laughed at her pranks and freely indulged her. If he did consider Rosamund had been neglectful he could at least have waited to reprimand her when they were alone. They all knew Lucie was not the reason for her presence at Belmont and he had never complained before. To so denigrate her before the supercilious French girl was both cruel and unjust, but what hurt her most was the suspicion that he wanted to show Madeleine of how little importance she was to him by humiliating her in her presence.

'Adela, take Lucie to bed,' he went on coldly. 'Miss Prescott, you'd better go to your room and,' a mischievous gleam came into his eyes, 'meditate upon your misdemeanours. Send Ellen to clear up this mess.' He indicated the spilt creams and powder. 'Madeleine, *ma chère*, let me take you downstairs and give you a drink.'

Madeleine hung back.

'I want them out of here before I go.'

'Naturally. Please to remove yourselves, all of you.'

Adela carried Lucie towards the door, apologising profusely as she went. Lucie, already recovering, shrilled:

'Want my dolly!'

Rosamund hastily picked it up from off the bed as Madeleine made a movement towards it with an expression that indicated that the toy would be massacred if she got her hands on it. She walked past Adrian and out of the room with lowered eyes and flushed cheeks, out-

raged dignity in every line of her slim body, aware of his
quizzical gaze upon her. She followed Adela into Lucie's
room and after sponging her face, settled her in her bed
with the doll beside her. Both forbore to scold. Lucie had
never been struck before in all her short life, and the experience had shattered her.

'I'll stay with her,' Rosamund offered, 'until she's
asleep. I know you've several oddments to attend to
downstairs and you have to send Ellen up.'

'I'll clear up the mess myself,' Mrs Grey decided. 'Then
I'll know it's done properly. Thank you, Miss Rosamund, she's nearly off now. I must say I'm surprised at
the Master, it wasn't your fault.'

'He seemed to think so,' Rosamund said bitterly. 'But
let's forget it.'

She knew she never would, but she did not want to
discuss the matter further with the housekeeper.

Adela went and Rosamund sat down in a low chair
beside the bed, while her burning resentment hardened
into resolution. She had taken all she could from Adrian
Belmont, and her position in his house had become un-
tenable. Confident that her sense of gratitude for benefits
received would keep her there, he thought he could treat
her as he pleased, but all said and done, she was there
primarily to give him the opportunity to fulfil a cherished
ambition and the privileges and presents he gave her
were to keep her sweet, but even so, he could not control
his capricious temper, as he had shown tonight, and
again in his behaviour over Tony. The ambition was a
little twisted, for he could only triumph vicariously
through her efforts and she had often been amazed at the
importance he attached to them. If she left him she could
still pursue her athletic career if she wished to do so and
find some employment that would allow her the neces-

sary free time, and leave him she would, for she was
weary of the emotional conflicts Adrian caused her, and
the coming of his fiancée, for that apparently was Madeleine's role, was a further aggravation. It would be a
wrench to leave Lucie, and ... she faced it honestly ...
Adrian himself, but it was the only way in which she
could find peace.

Lucie was sound asleep, and Rosamund could go now.
She would retire to her room, not to meditate upon her
misdoings as he had sarcastically bidden her but to
write out her formal notice. It would be easier that way.
Tomorrow being Saturday, Lucie would not be going to
school, and Adrian was taking the Delaneys to London
for the day, Mrs Grey had mentioned that when preparing the next day's menu. So the coast would be clear and
Rosamund would hire the local taxi to convey herself and
her gear to her home.

Her indignation was still white-hot and she wanted to
relieve it by writing her note before she slept, making it as
cold and cutting as she could.

She opened Lucie's door and stepping outside was
taken aback to find Adrian standing in the corridor a
few paces from her. The unexpected sight of him caused
her pulses to hammer, but she eyed him warily. Was he
waiting for her to give her a further scolding?

He took a step towards her. 'Is the brat all right?' he
asked. 'I came to see.'

'She's asleep.' There was no need to write what she
had to say, she could tell him now. 'Mr Belmont, can I
have a word with you alone?'

'That sounds ominous, but I should be returning to
my guests. Won't it keep?'

'*No!*' She was emphatic. 'I won't delay you long.' She

moved further along the corridor. 'I can tell you here and now.'

He glanced in some surprise at her pale resolute face.

'What's bitten you, Ros?' He smiled wryly. 'My behaviour has been exemplary as far as I'm aware.'

'It has not!' Her low voice quivered with repressed anger. 'Did you have to reprimand me so severely in front of Mrs Grey and ... and a stranger? If you thought I was to blame, couldn't you have waited until we were alone?'

'Surely you didn't take me seriously?' Laughter lines crinkled attractively around his eyes. 'I didn't blame you in the least. We all know what a young imp Lucie is. You couldn't have foreseen the mischief she was plotting.'

'Of course I couldn't,' Rosamund stammered, bewildered by this change of front. Involuntarily she was thinking she could not bear to leave him. His discerning gaze took in her agitation, her pallor and her wide eloquent eyes which were expressing far more than her lips would ever utter. She went on : 'But you said ...'

'Come off it, Ros.' His smile was devastating. No one could smile more charmingly than Adrian when he wanted to be disarming. 'Didn't you realise that was all an act put on to placate Miss Delaney? She expected me to reprove you, she believed you to be what she calls a *bonne*. It was not the moment to explain that you were my ... a very privileged person.'

'Am I?' She looked suddenly wistful. Adrian was trying to placate *her* now. Could he really be contemplating allying himself with that virago who could vent her spite so venomously on a little child? She wanted to beseech him to think again, to have more regard for his happiness, but it was not her affair, and after all, he could be vengeful himself.

'She behaved abominably to Lucie,' she declared.

'I agree, but we must be fair to her. It was distressing for her to have all her cosmetics rifled.' His eyes began to dance with merriment. 'A child using her precious unguents, which I know cost a pretty penny, to renovate a doll!' He began to laugh.

Unwillingly Rosamund smiled—the recent fracas had its comic side—and then finding Adrian's mirth infectious, she began to giggle.

'I'm afraid Mademoiselle Delaney didn't find it funny.'

'We could hardly expect her to, or poor little Lucie.' He became serious. 'Please try to keep her out of Madeleine's way, I know it won't be easy.'

'After tonight I imagine she'll have a wholesome awe of her,' Rosamund remarked drily. 'But what I wanted to tell you, Mr Belmont is that I've decided to go home.'

'Indeed? Are you parents ill, or do you want a holiday?'

'I meant for good.' But already she was hesitating. Their laughter had cleared the air and her grievances were fading.

'But that's absurd.' He took her by the shoulders and stared down into her eyes. 'What's the matter? Are you still offended because I scolded you? I was speaking to Miss Prescott, a somewhat legendary person, who, if she existed, would have accepted correction with becoming meekness. But you're my Ros, my golden girl, whose position here is unassailable. Madeleine doesn't know that yet, she'll understand when I explain.'

Rosamund was quite sure Madeleine would not understand. She said falteringly: 'I ... I'd rather you didn't discuss me with Mademoiselle Delaney.'

There was something mesmeric about Adrian's intent

blue gaze, he seemed to be looking into her very soul and her resolution was wavering.

'I must make your position clear to her.' His hands moved behind her back and he drew her close against him. 'Promise you won't leave me.'

'Mademoiselle Delaney certainly wouldn't understand if she saw us now,' Rosamund parried. Her every nerve was quivering at his touch. Did he know how he affected her and was he putting on another act to break down her resistance?

'Do you, I wonder?' he asked surprisingly, and repeated his question. 'Say you'll never leave me.'

'I . . . don't think I can.'

'That's better, but I want a definite promise. You always keep your word, don't you, Ros?'

His hand moved to the nape of her neck, pressing her face against his shoulder, and he laid his cheek against hers, lightly, caressingly. 'Promise, Ros,' he murmured in her ear.

Maddening, perverse, even dangerous—she could not withstand him. He moved her as no other man had ever done, or ever would. Her life would be desolate without him.

'You win,' she whispered. 'I'll stay . . . as long as you want me.'

'That'll be . . . for a long time yet.'

He touched her cheek with his lips, and withdrew his arms. 'Goodnight, golden girl, sleep well, and dream of . . . Olympic medals.'

He turned her about and pushed her towards her room. When she looked round he was a black shadow moving swiftly and silently down the length of the corridor, seeming unimpeded by his limp. Rosamund touched the place where his lips had caressed her. Unpredictable man, he had been so aloof until Lucie's escapade had produced this surprising aftermath. Perhaps with his uncanny perception he had sensed her rebellion and had come to her determined to forge anew the chains in which he held her, for he did not want to let her go until she had become in truth a golden girl.

With a sigh she went into her room, her original purpose discarded. Hate, love, indignation, reconciliation—it did not matter what she felt towards him, she was hopelessly in thrall to the Master of Belmont.

# CHAPTER SEVEN

LUCIE seemed none the worse for her previous night's adventure next morning. The graze caused by Madeleine's rings had already healed over. Healthy children recover fast. She seemed rather pleased with her achievement; her doll's rainbow-hued countenance, she insisted, was an improvement upon her former pallor.

'She looks as if she has scarlatina, smallpox and measles all at once,' was Rosamund's comment, which Lucie accepted with placid indifference. Nor could her grandmother wring from her any sign of penitence.

'She had lots and lots of little pots,' Lucie pointed out. 'I thinked she could let me have some.'

'But they weren't yours, and you'd no business in her room.'

'She left her door wide open,' Lucie averred. 'It *asked* me to go in.'

Mrs Grey had no way of disproving that and remarked that perhaps the door catch was faulty and she would check it when she took Mademoiselle Delaney's breakfast up to her, for the French girl preferred to have her dry toast and black coffee brought to her room.

Rosamund felt restless and was already half regretting her promise to Adrian. There was too much Delaney in the atmosphere at Belmont and she wanted to escape from it. After doing her room and Lucie's, she changed into sweater and shorts and went outside.

The sun had broken through the early morning mist and was spreading a golden glow over the frost-spangled turf, though white vapour was still gathered under the trees, that thrust their naked branches towards the pale blue sky. The nip in the air was invigorating, so that Rosamund was lured from the track into the vistas of the park.

It was a pagan morning that called to something primitive in her being buried beneath the layers of civilised living. She ran effortlessly over the short grass, her blood tingling with the sheer joy of being alive, the swift motion and a sense of her own power. She was not conscious of her limbs at all, nor of shortness of breath, she seemed to be flying. She loved to run like this, untrammelled by stopwatches or calculations of distances covered, as naturally as a bird flies or a wild creature flees, rejoicing in her own fleetness and the beauty of the morning.

She circled the park, and as she returned towards the track two rust-red canine shapes rushed to join her, imbued with the same effervescence that bubbled in her veins, barking gleefully.

'Come on, boys!' she called, and girl and dogs raced towards home at a speed that would have won them a world record.

There were two figures waiting beside the track, watching her approach, who had evidently come in search of her.

'Diana and her hounds,' Adrian said as she reached them. Once Rosamund had remarked upon his fondness for such allusions, and he had laughed and said she must blame it on a classical education. This morning the simile was apt; her white-clad, long-legged form with the two dogs beside her looked like an illustration from Greek mythology. The dogs were panting, pink tongues lolling, but Rosamund was not even winded.

Adrian and Madeleine had obviously been riding, for they were both dressed for that exercise, and their clothes became them. Adrian looked spruce in breeches, boots, sweater and hacking jacket, and jodhpurs suited Madeleine's slim height. They were beautifully cut and so were the smart waistcoat and jacket she wore with them. She had a white stock at her throat and a hard hat upon her head. She might have been going into the show ring.

By contrast Rosamund looked undressed, and Madeleine's eyes dwelt upon her bare knees.

'Are you not frozen?' she asked.

Rosamund's exhilaration faded under her companions' critical stares.

'I've been running,' she pointed out, 'so I don't feel cold, and it's a gorgeous morning.'

Madeleine said stiltedly: 'I appear to have been under a misapprehension regarding your status, Miss Prescott. I did not know you were Mr Belmont's protégée, not Lucie's *bonne*.'

Her small eyes studied Rosamund insolently as she spoke, and Rosamund shot a quick glance at Adrian. He had lost no time in explaining her position to Madeleine and he smiled reassuringly as the other girl went on:

'It is to me a strange custom to take a *jeune fille* under one's protection to teach her to run and not ...' She hesitated.

'Sleep with her,' Adrian finished for her with a wicked grin. 'But we're British, Madeau, and venerate sport too much to mix it with ... er ... other pleasures. Have you finished, Ros, or may we see you in action?'

'I hadn't intended to do any more,' Rosamund told him.

'Not even to show Mademoiselle Delaney that you

really do run?' There was a gibe in his voice, as if there had been some argument about that.

'Not even to do that,' Rosamund returned sweetly, but she was outraged by the implication that her training was a cover-up to conceal her true position. The magic had gone out of the morning, and she had no inclination to jog round the track for Madeleine's edification.

The dogs created a diversion by brushing against Madeleine's jodhpurs.

'*Mon dieu*, but they're wet!' she squealed. 'Adrian, do not let them ruin my clothes!'

'They won't hurt them,' Adrian declared unsympathetically, but he called the dogs to heel.

The trio walked back towards the house, while Madeleine chattered vivaciously. She had an amusing turn of phrase and made them both laugh. When she was animated her eyes sparkled and her thin face glowed. Rosamund had to admit that she had a gamine charm when she chose to exert it, which together with her salty wit would appeal to a man satiated by more obvious attractions, and Adrian seemed to enjoy her company. They parted at the house, host and guest to enter by the imposing front door, Rosamund to scuttle round to the side, reflecting that riding was the one sport Adrian still enjoyed and Madeleine had the advantage of being able to share it with him. She herself knew nothing about horses, though she had often admired the two handsome creatures he kept in the Belmont stables—but from a distance. Adrian had never suggested matching her with his horses, she thought whimsically, and it would be a pleasant change to be carried on their backs instead of depending upon her own locomotion.

The Delaneys departed with their host before lunch upon their planned expedition and Rosamund took Lucie

with her to the Crystal Palace track in the afternoon with
a supply of books to keep her amused while she ran; but
owing to her exuberance of the early morning, plus the
turmoil of the night before, she ran badly. Adrian was
quite right, emotion did play havoc with form. She must
banish him and his lady love firmly to the back of her
mind and remember that she was first and foremost an
athlete.

On Monday morning Adrian accompanied her down
to the Belmont track to see, he said, how she had improved. Brutally he told her she must have been slacking,
since she had not done so at all. He proceeded to drive
her with almost sadistic intensity, so that she wondered if
Madeleine had refused him and he was taking it out on
her. He allowed her barely a few minutes for recovery before he sent her off again on another sprint, and he did
not permit her to stop until she was completely exhausted.
Hitherto she had always obeyed his orders implicitly
when they related to athletics, trusting to his judgment,
but that morning she was on the verge of mutiny. She was
not going to let him vent his ill temper on her for Madeleine's obduracy, but she was so weary she did not go
beyond a few reproachful looks, which he ignored,
though she resolved if he repeated the performance she
would protest loudly and vehemently before she reached
her present state of tiredness.

He did not. The following day he was sunny and
almost considerate. He even complimented her.

'Get another half second off your time and you'll be
in championship class,' he told her, waving his stopwatch.

The four hundred metres, roughly a quarter of a mile,
was Rosamund's best distance. The difference between
a record and an average time was only a matter of sec-

onds, or even fractions of seconds could be vital. The race was run under a minute, and that one minute could be the most momentous in her whole life.

Though he was spending more time with her in the mornings, Adrian spent the rest of his day with the Delaneys. Rosamund never had any contact with Madame Delaney; she appeared to be a semi-invalid, lying in bed late, and when she did get up, sitting by the fire in the drawing room, either reading or sewing. But she encountered Madeleine frequently either in the house or out in the grounds. The French girl even came into the housekeeper's room to talk to Mrs Grey and to make her peace with Lucie. She gave the little girl a rouge pot, which the child promptly applied to her own face and was furious when her grandmother made her wash it off.

'Mademoiselle Delaney seems to poking her nose into everything,' Rosamund said disgustedly, for Madeleine seemed to be making an inventory of the house and contents. Mrs Grey defended her.

'Since she expects to live here, it's only natural she should be interested in how the place is run and what amenities it possesses. She probably has alterations in mind. She has all a Frenchwoman's thrift and confided in me that she considers the master is far too extravagant.'

'Isn't that rather impertinent?' Rosamund asked drily, for Madeleine seemed to be taking a lot for granted without having yet obtained her engagement ring.

'Not at all. She anticipates being mistress here and she's no romantic teenager. Her outlook is entirely practical. She'll make the Master a most efficient wife.'

'I hope he appreciates it. I rather think Mr Belmont likes to run things his own way. Besides ...' Rosamund broke off. This talk of thrift and practicality seemed terribly cold-blooded, and not the right approach to marriage. Didn't love come into it at all, or was Adrian past it? Perhaps he would prefer a well organised home to emotional raptures, since he was so mistrustful of deep feelings. As for Madeleine, she did not act like a girl in love at all. Was it Belmont House she was after?

As if guessing what was in her mind, Adela told her:

'The French consider marriage mainly as a business contract, or so I'm told, and the Master is beyond a boy's infatuation. It's enough that they're compatible, and Dr Delaney, being well off, will give his daughter a substantial marriage portion. Mark my words, we'll soon be hearing wedding bells.'

'They'll be too far off if the wedding takes place in France.'

'It probably will, and I hope Mr Belmont will arrange for me to attend it, but I'm sure he will seeing that I've known them all, his father and his grandfather, black Belmonts all, proud and passionate . . .' The housekeeper embarked upon a sea of reminiscences.

There did not seem to be much passion involved in this alliance, Rosamund thought. She knew Adrian was capable of it, but his attitude towards Madeleine was cool; as for the latter, she looked unlikely to be swayed by it, though she could be violently vindictive.

Days passed and spring approached. Madame Delaney was much better and talking about going home, but still Adrian had not declared himself. He seemed much more interested in Rosamund's fixtures, for the season would start in May. Britain was waking up to the fact that it was Olympics year and there were other sports besides Soccer. Rosamund was sure that Adrian would not get married until after the Olympiad in October, but there was nothing to prevent him becoming engaged. Why was he stalling? Even when the visitors had fixed the

date for their return, no announcement was made,
though it was possible that the couple had a secret understanding. Rosamund thought Madeleine wanted to tell
her that, when one evening, a few days before her departure, she knocked upon her bedroom door, and asked
if she could speak to her in private.

Rosamund had not begun to undress; she was sitting
by the small electric fire with which she had been provided, pleasantly relaxed after the day's toil. She got to
her feet when her visitor came in, wondering what ordeal
lay ahead of her. Madeleine wore an evening gown, a
golden sheath, with jewels about her throat and in her
ears. The colour recalled to Rosamund that she had not
yet returned Adrian's topaz necklace. It would go well
with Madeleine's dress, and it was to her it would go if
she surrendered it. Instantly she decided to keep it. It was
a memento of a lovely Christmas until Adrian had spoilt
it by his jealousy or whatever had motivated him. And
that episode had become pale in retrospect.

Rosamund offered her chair to her visitor and perched
herself on her bed, while Madeleine looked appraisingly
around the comfortable room.

'Your quarters are quite luxurious for a nursemaid,'
Madeleine observed languidly. 'But then you're much
more than that, *n'est-ce pas*. Miss Prescott?' Her eyes
glittered like jet beads. '*Moi*, I am broad-minded, but I
do not like there should be gossip about *mon cher ami*.'

'Is there gossip?' Rosamund asked, perceiving from
whence the attack was coming.

Madeleine shrugged her narrow shoulders. 'Are you so
naïve? Or is it a pretence? There is always gossip about
Mr Belmont. He is wealthy, attractive, a bachelor, and,
*hélas*, so indiscreet! He flouts convention, allowing that
child to be brought up here. True, he denies paternity,

but who believes him? He indulges her shamefully—she was not punished for the damage she did in my room.' Evidently that had rankled. 'But I only mention Lucie as an example of his folly. It is of another matter I wish to speak.'

She looked at Rosamund narrowly, and the girl returned her gaze unflinchingly. There could not have been a greater contrast between two women—Rosamund, with her large eyes and candid open face, her slim lithe body, in which the muscles rippled under the smooth skin, and the French girl, all angles and sharp points, with her secret malicious smile. She went on:

'*Maintenant*, he tells the world he is coaching you to be a champion sprinter, so far permissible, but he keeps you in his house on the pretext of caring for the child. Does he think we are all fools? He coaches no one else, and is interested only in you ... wherefore? Because you are exceptional? *Mon dieu*, you're no better than many another.'

She leaned forward, her black eyes piercing in the intensity of her gaze. 'What do you hope to achieve, Miss Prescott? Surely you know that Mr Belmont would never marry you, though you were the fastest runner in the world, which you are not.'

'Good God, I never thought of such a thing!' Rosamund exclaimed, so startled that her voice rang with sincerity. 'I thought he was going to marry you.'

Madeleine seemed discomfited by this frank admission. She moved in her chair so that the glow from the fire caused the folds of her dress to ripple like the coils of a snake. She was not unlike a snake, Rosamund thought, with her small head on which the hair lay flat and her jewel-bright eyes.

'We have an understanding,' she said haughtily, which

was what Rosamund had supposed. Then her calm broke
into irritation. 'I have to take Madame Delaney home,
and Adrian refuses to come with us because of this
*bêtise* about athletics. Mr Belmont was a great athlete in
his time, but he's a back number now. I have tried to
persuade him that you would do better under a professional coach, but he says you depend upon him. You
should free him from that obligation, Miss Prescott, for
you're becoming something of a burden to him.'

Recalling his insistence in the corridor when Adrian
had made her promise never to leave him, Rosamund
could afford to smile.

'You haven't got your facts quite right,' she told her. 'I
did suggest ... er ... a change, but Mr Belmont refused
to release me.'

Venom glinted in Madeleine's narrowed eyes.

'Are you sure you did not misunderstand him?' Rosamund shook her head, and Madeleine changed her tac-
tics.

'Does he realise you are emotionally involved with
him?' she asked softly. 'That doesn't help a budding
athlete. I myself have skied for France, so I know of
what I speak. You will strive to achieve miracles to impress him, but he will grow tired of you, for a man can't
absorb himself in one girl's career for ever. When he
withdraws his support, you will collapse. A sad history,
but inevitable. You can avoid it if you are wise.'

It was only to be expected that Madeleine was jealous
of Adrian's interest in his protégée, she was obviously a
possessive woman, but though there was some truth in
her assertions, Rosamund was not going to admit it.

'What makes you think I'm emotionally involved with
Mr Belmont?' She tried to speak carelessly, but two

bright spots of colour rose in her cheeks. Madeleine looked at her pityingly.

'*Ma chère*, you are as transparent as glass.'

Involuntarily Rosamund winced. Oh no, she thought, if she can read me, so must he—but what was there to read? Her feelings towards Adrian were still in a state of chaos. When he was sarcastic and domineering, she hated him, but when she thought of leaving him, she believed she loved him. He both repelled and fascinated her, but she had had no real experience of love, her feelings for Tony had been a placid pond compared with the whirlpool of her reactions to Adrian. One thing she did know, she could never be indifferent to him, and she did not want him to marry Madeleine Delaney.

Madeleine watched the play of emotion across the girl's expressive face. Cold and calculating herself, she could appreciate that Rosamund's was a warmer, more impulsive nature, and open to exploitation, so she sought to rouse in her a sense of self-preservation.

'You will only be hurt if you stay here,' she went on, 'for you can expect nothing from Mr Belmont. He is far too shrewd to allow you to compromise him.' Which seemed to contradict her earlier statements. 'No doubt you've dreamed of being the mistress of Belmont, it would be a wonderful thing for a *petite bourgeoise* as you are, and you hope your running prowess will provide the bait. You move beautifully when you run, I have watched you through Mr Belmont's field glasses, but that is not enough. Nor will your big eyes nor your golden hair catch him, for you are too young, too crude, too naïve. Adrian Belmont looks for good breeding in his wife, elegance and *savoir-faire*, to say nothing of a *dot*.'

'Quite so,' Rosamund said drily, amused by this mingling of flattery and denigration. 'I've never had any pretensions regarding Mr Belmont, Miss Delaney, believe it or not as you please. He has no personal feelings towards me, only this whim, you might call it, to create an Olympic runner. He considers me promising material, that's all there is to it.'

But what of the night when he had kissed her and coaxed her? Had that been all an act?

'Such a situation between a man and a woman is unnatural.' Madeleine was equally dry. 'Though he will never ask you to be his wife, and he cannot do that unless he repudiates me, which I would never permit, he will eventually make you his mistress.'

Rosamund's eyes blazed amber fire in her pale face, but she controlled her temper.

'You jump to unjustifiable conclusions, Miss Delaney, but I wonder you can suggest such a thing, for such an action would be an insult to yourself. Don't you trust Mr Belmont?'

Madeleine shrugged her shoulders. 'Men being men, I don't expect the impossible. You'll be the one on the spot, unless I can persuade you to leave. You constitute a danger to me, yourself and to him.'

'You exaggerate. I'm not a poacher and Mr Belmont is an honourable man.'

'Human nature is human nature,' Madeleine returned tritely. She looked towards the fire and for an instant her hard face softened. 'I have known Adrian for years, he was a wonderful person before his accident embittered him—*si gentil, si beau*. When he ran he looked like the god Mercury in flight. And he loved me, I was so proud.'

'Yet when he was smashed up, you didn't come to him.'

'Who told you that?' Madeleine drew back her head like a serpent about to strike. 'I am not an imbecile,' she went on as Rosamund did not reply, unwilling to mention Mrs Grey. 'I thought he might become a cripple.'

Rosamund registered shocked reproach and Madeleine laughed shrilly.

'One must be realistic, *mon amie*. Imagine life tied to a man in a wheelchair.'

'But if that man was Adrian,' Rosamund protested, using in her agitation his first name.

'Mr Belmont to you, upstart!' Madeleine spat. 'I suppose you would have rushed to his side.'

'I would,' Rosamund said, simply and revealingly.

'Being a romantic idiot, but then Belmont House would have compensated you.'

'Didn't it appeal to you?'

'No, because I prefer to live in France. When we are married, Mr Belmont will join me there. This house is only fit to live in in the summer. We will visit it from time to time and most of it can be shut up or loaned for conferences. He says that Grey woman must be provided for, so she can stay on as caretaker.'

Madeleine had got it all taped. Rosamund, who knew Adrian loved his home, wondered if he had really agreed to the French girl's plans. Perhaps that was why he had stalled.

'*Eh bien*, I suppose I must wait for him to recover from this Olympic idiocy,' Madeleine sighed. She stood up, shaking out her long skirts. 'I came to speak to you, Miss Prescott, for your own good, but I find you impertinent and obdurate. I repeat, your aspirations are quite hopeless.'

'But I haven't got any,' Rosamund insisted.

'I think you lie,' Madeleine returned calmly. 'You still hope to trap him and so you cling like a limpet, but you don't know Adrian Belmont as well as I do. His heart atrophied when he was injured, but he'll break yours.'

With which dire prophecy she glided out of the room, closing the door firmly behind her, leaving Rosamund more elated than depressed. Much of what Madeleine had said was true, but it was what she had not said that was significant. Though she had implied that Adrian was going to marry her, she had been unable to announce that they were actually engaged and she did not wear his ring. Her efforts to oust Rosamund were prompted by fear of the influence which she had derided. She had to go and leave the field clear for her supposed rival and that had made her venomous.

Rosamund was confirmed in her conviction that Adrian would not commit himself until after the Olympics, and a whole summer stretched before them until that event, so she could for the time being dismiss the Delaneys from her mind.

When the Delaneys departed and still no announcement had been made, Mrs Grey frankly expressed her disappointment.

'What do you think went wrong?' she asked Rosamund. 'I thought that was what she came for.' She ruminated for a while. 'Is it possible she refused him? After all, he's a bit crotchety and he's lame.'

'That wouldn't make any difference if she loved him,' Rosamund told her. She was doubtful herself if Madeleine had ever loved Adrian. She had been flattered by his attentions when they had first met, and she had said he had loved her, but never suggested such a sentiment was returned. As for Adrian, he was as usual enigmatical, but Rosamund thought if the marriage did take place it would be one of convenience.

'Mr Belmont once told me he wasn't a marrying man,' she went on. 'Perhaps that's the truth.'

'Some men don't know what's good for them,' Adela said tartly.

'I don't think Miss Delaney would be very good for Mr Belmont,' Rosamund declared. 'The sort of woman he ought to marry should be pliant and clinging; she's too hard and self-assertive. One who would submit to being ruled by his stronger personality.' And she sighed, for she did not consider she was pliant and clinging either.

'In other words, a doormat,' Mrs Grey suggested. 'You're wrong there, Miss Rosamund, he likes a bit of spirit.' Her brow crinkled thoughtfully. 'Forgive my saying so, she didn't like you being here.'

'That was obvious, but it wasn't my fault. I'd have gone if Mr Belmont had dismissed me.'

'He'd never do that.' Mrs Grey continued to look at Rosamund as if another and not very pleasing idea had occurred to her. Oh dear, Rosamund thought, is she going to start on me now? To divert her, she said :

'She also resented Lucie.'

'Lucie has every right to be here,' Adela said vehemently, and Rosamund stared at her in dismay, for she would have staked her life upon Adrian's integrity. Mrs Grey laughed.

'No, no, Miss Rosamund, don't go getting me wrong. She's not his, but he had a young cousin staying here, he *has* got relatives, though none of them get along together. Well, young Barney, he was a racing driver, and a hellcat if ever there was one. All the worst of the Belmonts came out in him. My girl Ella was housemaid here then, and he fair turned her head. He killed himself before he could right her in the Grand Prix, but the Master felt

responsible for Lucie—after all, she is a Belmont, though
on the wrong side of the blanket as they say. When Ella
married Greg and he didn't want the poor mite, the
Master took her in and said he would always provide for
her, and so he will, whoever he marries.'

'But there has been gossip?' asked Rosamund.

'The Master doesn't care a snap of his fingers for gossip.'

'Mademoiselle Delaney does.'

Mrs Grey nodded her head. 'Yes, and when she's mistress here, Lucie and myself must live elsewhere, but the
Master will arrange it.'

Adela had complete confidence in Adrian, and Rosamund noticed she had said 'when', not 'if' Madeleine
came to Belmont, so she must still be certain that he
would eventually marry her.


Spring came and Rosamund's training was intensified.
Her best distances were the hundred metres and the four
hundred metres; she ran the latter in 52.1 seconds, which
was Lillian Board's time in the Mexico Olympics, but
that was some years ago. They decided to concentrate on
these two races, with perhaps an occasional attempt to
run the eight hundred metres.

May came, bringing the County Championships, and
Rosamund was running two or three races a week and
winning them all. She had her own collection of trophies
and cups. She ran under the auspices of the South
London club she had originally belonged to, but everyone knew she was Adrian Belmont's latest find and he
was coaching her. She earned the soubriquet of 'The
Belmont Bomb'. June brought her first trip abroad, to
run in Sweden, and she returned victorious.

Adrian attended all her races, sitting or standing where

she could see him if she turned her head. Though she could not always distinguish him if it were a big stadium, she was always conscious of his presence, his strength and encouragement reaching out to her. At only one meeting was he missing. He had gone for a weekend to Haute Savoie, and upon that occasion Rosamund ran badly, finishing fourth. He did not tell her he was going to visit Madeleine until the day before, and her sense of desolation when she knew he would not be there must have accounted for her poor performance. Many athletes become dependent upon their coaches for guidance and correction, but in Rosamund's case it amounted to obsession. But though Adrian was always there in the background, except upon that one occasion, she was never alone with him. Most of her training now was done at the Crystal Palace track as she needed competitors to pace her. It had been arranged for a school bus to pick up Lucie, so Rosamund had sole use of the Mini in which to travel. Adrian would drop in at her meetings when it suited him, coming in his own car and mingling with his acquaintances.

There were no Empire games that summer, for the coming Olympics overshadowed all else.

Rosamund's progress was one big question mark. Her times were excellent, but it was only her second season and she had not had much experience of big events. Could she hold her own against the black Atalantas and East European Amazons who were expected to mop up all the medals in the Olympics? The sports commentators speculated, and Adrian, who sometimes appeared on television, answered with an affirmative. Rosamund herself he shielded from publicity as much as possible.

'I want to keep them guessing,' he told her. 'You don't need a build-up, your performance will speak for itself.'

When the names for the British team were announced hers was included, an unpopular selection, since there were others who thought they had a better claim than Adrian Belmont's practically unknown protégée, whom they considered an outsider.

'But they hadn't run faster than 53.2,' Adrian told Rosamund, being in the know. The matter of one second could make all the difference.

Rosamund was jubilant, she had dreaded that she might not be selected, but Adrian did not seem surprised.

'The selectors are not fools,' he told her blandly. 'Mind you justify their choice. You'll be running for Britain, remember.'

Which did not excite her at all. She was running for Adrian Belmont, to win for him an Olympic gold, and that was her motive.

'Will Miss Delaney be there?' she asked with apparent inconsequence.

Adrian looked surprised at her question. 'Of course, they'll all be there. Dr Delaney is fanatical about althletics. Why do you ask?'

'Oh, I just wondered.'

So Madeleine would be among the spectators. Now it was more than ever imperative that she won.

# CHAPTER EIGHT

SAN ANTONIO, capital of a Central American state, normally of little interest to the peoples of the West except the tourists, became that October the focus of the eyes of the sporting world, for there would be gathered the élite among the athletes of the globe in the hope of winning laurels for their country, men and women of every colour of skin.

A vast Olympic stadium had been erected on its outskirts, with its attendant swimming pools, playing fields, radio and television centres and the Olympic village to house the competitors, a small town in itself. The city was situated in a hollow and ringed by ranges of mountains that had been there long before man began to dominate the earth, whose snow-clad peaks rose skywards in lofty disdain of the activities of the hordes of human ants scurrying about at their feet.

Rosamund flew there with the British team, but since Adrian did not belong to it, he would be travelling independently and staying in the city with the Delaneys, as he informed her with a wry grin as if he suspected her feelings about that—or perhaps he meant it as a goad. She knew no other arrangement was possible, for she would stay at the Olympic village, but when he saw her off at the airport she wished with all her heart that he had been accompanying her, he gave her strength and confidence among this crowd of strangers all intent upon their own hopes and fears.

She had been entered for two events, the four hundred

and the short sprint of a hundred metres. The team manager told her frankly she had not much hope of a place—perhaps with luck the bronze. She would be running against Lola Smithson, a girl from Kenya who up to now had been unbeaten. She was a hot favourite for the gold, and would be running in both her events and the eight hundred metres.

'She isn't human,' he said gloomily. 'A dynamo on two legs.'

Anna Cornish, a Canadian, was backed for the silver, a superb sprinter who had won the Empire Games medals the previous year. Rosamund was something of an outsider and she tried not to be daunted by his obvious doubt of her abilities.

She had seen Lola run on television, an effortless win, but her time had been only a second less than her own best personal, and by the law of averages she had to be beaten sometime.

The Opening of the Games seemed to her like a fantastic dream, so much colour, noise and spectacle. Rosamund marched into the stadium with the rest of the team, following her country's flag, wearing the short pleated skirt and red blazer that had been designed for the girls that year. The colour did not suit her, because it clashed with her red-gold hair. She knew Adrian must be somewhere in the crowded stands—with Madeleine— but it was quite impossible to distinguish him. She walked proudly, bearing herself well but without elation. She was there because Adrian wanted her to be there, but she would far rather be in the park at Belmont, running with the dogs.

She stood among the massed pack of athletes in the arena, finding it unpleasantly hot, although it was October. The somewhat trite speeches passed over her head, high-sounding phrases about honour, the amateur ideal, the linking of nations through sport. Then the runner, a lithe bronze-hued youth in white, brought the torch in to the track and nimbly mounted the long stairway to the plinth and dipped the torch into the bowl. The flame shot up and the Games were open.

Rosamund found Adrian waiting for her when she returned to the Olympic village, standing outside the women's block where she was to lodge. Vaguely she wondered how he had managed to be there. No one was admitted without a pass and security was strict. But Adrian was internationally known and would have no difficulty in gaining entry where he would.

'Oh, Adrian, I'm so glad to see you!' she exclaimed, her whole face lighting up.

He smiled sardonically. 'Feeling as if I'd thrown you to the wolves?' he enquired. 'Or lions would be more appropriate. *Ave Caesar, morituri te salutant* ... those about to die salute you ... but at least you won't be executed if you're defeated.'

She laughed shakily. 'If I am, I'd like to be.'

'Ros, my darling, you're being morbid. This is only a game, not a matter of life and death.'

But it was to her, and to many of them there; in her case if she did not win Adrian's gold medal she might as well die. She was too strung up to think rationally, and noticing that, he looked at her a little anxiously.

'Keep cool, old girl, you'll be all right,' he told her confidently. 'You're running your heat for the hundred metres in the morning, aren't you?'

She confirmed that. Adrian was wearing a cream-coloured blazer with white flannels and an open-necked shirt, and carried an ebony stick with a silver knob. With his black hair and deeply burned skin he looked

slightly foreign, a grand Señor from former days. He told
her that he would be sitting in the stadium on the front
row near the starting point so she could identify him.

'And to make sure of that, I'll wave this.'

He shook out a bright green square with a gold lion
rampant printed upon it—the lion rampant Rosamund
had been told had been the crest of the Belmont family
when they had borne arms, which they no longer did.
Adrian declared that armorial bearings were outdated
and ostentatious.

'A bit of Belmont in Latin America,' she exclaimed,
touched by his thoughtfulness. He must have guessed
how much she relied upon his support and the sight of
him would cheer her.

'What will Miss Delaney think of that?' she added.

'What should she think? She's not your trainer,' he
countered. 'Anyway, she won't be sitting near me, says
it's too hot and noisy in the front. There are awnings
further back to give some shade. The sun never bothers
me.'

Information that pleased Rosamund still more. She
had felt that this Olympiad was something she wanted to
share only with Adrian and the French girl's presence
would be an intrusion, but if she was well to the back she
could be forgotten.

'Let's go to the canteen and get something to eat,' he
went on. 'You must be ravenous after all that standing
about.'

As Rosamund walked with Adrian to the dining room
it was as if sunlight had broken through a dark cloud,
but it was not only her depression that the sight of him
had dispelled, but in a sudden moment of illumination,
her mixed feelings regarding him had coalesced into the
realisation that she loved him, deeply and irrevocably;

had loved him for a long while, else she would never have suffered those upsurges of burning hate, which were the reverse side of love. She had had to come half across the world before she could bring herself to admit the truth of her emotions. The ordeal she was about to face was wholly on his account, for though she had been endowed with the shape and speed for running, she was not naturally competitive, and it was Adrian's ambition and drive that had brought her to San Antonio. If she could have followed her own inclinations, she would have gone back to England on the next plane.

But she was here and pledged to compete, so that the simile to the ancient gladiators was not inapt. She was about to go into battle for Adrian's sake. Who had called her a sacrifice upon Adrian Belmont's altar? Tony, who was jealous of her association with him. But Tony Bridges was not here today, he had not qualified, being one of Adrian's few failures, and it was up to her to justify all the time and effort her coach had expended upon her.

Although the dining room was crowded, they might have been alone for all the notice anyone took of them. It was thronged with athletes of every nationality, runners, jumpers, discus throwers and other sportsmen, but none of the British team seemed to be present. All about them rose the babble of different tongues. Those sitting nearest to them were Russians, understanding little English and speaking less. They paid no attention to the dark distinguished-looking man and the glowing girl after one cursory glance. For Rosamund was glowing with the newly discovered wonder of her love and her dedication of it to the man opposite her. She felt the exaltation of a pagan priestess before the altar of her god. So stimulated she could not fail, while as for Mademoiselle Delaney, she did not give her a thought. This was her hour.

Adrian's eyes dwelt upon her with appreciation. She had rarely looked more lovely, her amber eyes luminous in a face that seemed translucent with the stress of her emotions, the spirit shining through the flesh. She had discarded her blazer and her white dress had a sacrificial purity, while her red-gold hair might have been an aureole.

'Nervous about tomorrow?' he asked.

She shook her head. 'It's only a heat. I know I'll qualify.'

'Of course you will, and there's no need to push yourself until the final.'

Some of her elation faded as she thought of that. 'I'll have to meet Lola Smithson in the final if not before. She's supposed to be invincible.'

'She's built up a legend, but nobody is invincible, and though she may beat you in the hundred metres, she's got a spring like a panther, she won't in the four hundred. That's always been your best distance, and your times are equal to hers.'

He was dealing out the confidence and reassurance that every athlete needs before a competition. Rosamund was not unduly perturbed; Lola Smithson was formidable opposition, but she was sure she could beat her with so much at stake. But when the Olympiad was finished, what then? Her bright face clouded as the darkened future loomed before her.

'When it's all over,' she said uncertainly, 'what do I do then?'

'What do you mean, when it's all over?' he demanded. His blue gaze met hers searchingly. 'It'll never be all over between you and me, Ros. You don't suppose your victory will end our association?'

His expression caused her heart to quicken and a wild hope was born.

'If I win the gold ... isn't that all you've ever wanted from me?' she asked, and waited, every nerve tensed, for his reply.

'No, Ros, I want much more than that from you.' He laid his hand over hers on the table and she looked down at his long brown fingers, waiting with bated breath for him to continue. Did dreams sometimes come true? Was this Olympiad the prelude to winning what was worth far more than gold?

'You've become part of my life,' he said softly. 'I can't imagine Belmont without you now, the sunshine would have gone from it.' He grinned suddenly, impishly. 'I knew when I first saw you trespassing in my park that you meant trouble, and so you did. I haven't known a peaceful moment since.'

Rosamund did not know quite how to take this observation; the latter part seemed to contradict the first. She said doubtfully:

'My training must have taken up a lot of your time.'

'I'm not talking about running, Ros,' he told her earnestly. 'That was incidental, a means to keep you with me.' She stared at him wide-eyed. Did he know what he was saying? Or had the hot sun affected him? He had insisted so often that he only tolerated her because he was interested in her athletic talent.

'But you're so young,' he went on with a short sigh. 'Twenty-one, isn't it, to my thirty. Thirty is quite a milestone, but the gap isn't unbridgeable if ...' He broke off and stared absently at the broad back of a discus thrower. 'Miracles can happen,' he concluded.

Rosamund was puzzled by the termination of this utterance. Its trend delighted her—at last Adrian was seeing her as a woman, a desirable woman, that was a miracle from her point of view, but it was not what he meant. Could he be referring to her coming victory? But he had just been assuring her that that was a certainty. Scrutinising his face, she found it more lucid than his words, and meeting the ardour in his eyes, she cried impulsively:

'Oh, Adrian, you're the most important thing in my life, in fact you *are* my life.'

He smiled crookedly and his clasp tightened upon her fingers.

'That's nice to know, my sweet, but it could be better put. Are you too shy to say "I love you"?' His voice had dropped to a low murmur, and hot colour rose to Rosamund's cheeks. So he had guessed her feelings, perhaps had known them better than she had done herself. Experienced with lovelorn women, he knew all the signs. She said almost challengingly:

'What if I do? Isn't a neophyte supposed to adore her master?'

'I don't want to be your master but your mate, and a neophyte sounds so chilly, moonlit shrines and that sort of thing.'

Blue flame flickered in the depths of his eyes, but Rosamund straightened herself in her seat and firmly withdrew her hand.

'Aren't you forgetting Miss Delaney?' she demanded frigidly.

He laughed. 'How you do harp on poor old Madeau! Has she been telling you fairy tales? If so I assure you I've given her no foundation for them—it's her father, Doctor Delaney, who's my friend.' Rosamund's heart leapt with joy at this assertion. Smiling whimsically, he concluded: 'Madeau can't win Olympic medals for me.'

'Didn't she ski in the Winter Olympics?'

'That was some time ago and she didn't do as well as she pretends to her friends—but why are we wasting precious time talking about her?'

Putting his elbows on the table and resting his chin on his raised hands, Adrian stared at Rosamund intently, his eyes sparkling like sapphires.

'When this is all over, Ros, I'm going to take you away with me. We'll dodge the English winter by going somewhere that's always summer. A Caribbean island perhaps—white sand, palm trees, the lot. The sort of place I bet you've often dreamed of but have never thought to visit. You'll run on the warm sands in only a bikini, with the sun gilding your body and your hair, a nereid, a sea nymph ... my classics again!' He smiled charmingly. 'We'll create our own Eden, just you and me.'

'Just you and me,' she echoed, caught by the magic of his words, and never have four syllables sounded more sweet. She did not care what his intentions towards her were; sufficient that he wanted to be with her. She had nothing to gain by preaching morality and everything to lose.

'You're very trusting, darling,' he mocked her gently. 'Aren't you afraid I'm trying to seduce you?'

'No,' she told him steadily. 'I'll settle for whatever you are prepared to offer. All I want is for us to be together.'

He changed his position, and picking up her hand raised it to his lips, lightly kissing her finger tips, to the great interest of a marathon runner who chanced to look over his shoulder to witness the gesture.

'I'd never do you wrong, darling,' Adrian told her, 'but before I propose properly ...' A shadow crossed his face and he dropped her hand. The runner looked disappointed and turned back to his colleagues. 'The miracle must happen.'

Rosamund looked at him questioningly. He must be referring to winning a gold medal, though that could hardly be termed a miracle, but she could think of nothing else that could come under that category. Since he did not seem to be going to elucidate, she said firmly:

'I'll not disappoint you.'

She could not lose now, she was on the crest of the wave. She would defeat not only Lola Smithson but Madeleine as well.

'That's my Golden Girl!' Adrian spoke absently as if his thoughts had already travelled elsewhere. His regard had left her face and he was staring into space, as if he had forgotten her presence.

'Adrian!' she sought to recall him.

His eyes switched back to her, and he smiled reassuringly.

'You'd better get some rest, my darling.' They stood up and he touched her cheek gently with his finger tip. 'I'll be in the stadium tomorrow morning to see you run your heat.'

They parted at the entrance to the women's quarters, and as she watched him walk away, it seemed to Rosamund that he leaned more heavily on his stick and his limp was more pronounced. Was it only by contrast with the strong, firm limbs of the athletes surrounding her? His disability made no difference to her love for him, rather it increased it, but would their fitness pain him because he had wanted so much to run himself in an Olympiad? But it would seem he was at last coming to terms with his injury and was prepared to lead a normal married life in spite of it. For the implication behind his flowery talk was plain; he had conquered his reluctance to assume the matrimonial yoke and when she had won her race he would ask her to marry him. It seemed almost unbelievable, but what else could she think? She felt both humble and elated.

That night Rosamund stood at the window, while her room-mate—they were accommodated in pairs—slept soundly in her bed. She gazed for a long time up at the great white stars blazing in a purple pall above the snow-clad summits of the mountain crests that showed silver in the starshine. Life was wonderful. Almost at the same moment that she had come to the full realisation of her love for Adrian, she had learned that it was reciprocated, or so it appeared after what he had said. She felt strong and uplifted, confident that nothing could defeat her now, for with the great surge of joy and happiness surging through her veins she would be invincible. Adrian's miracle would come to pass.

Rosamund did not meet Lola Smithson until the final of the hundred metres. She won her heat and the semi-final with seconds in hand, beating, to her great glee, the East German champion. She came full of confidence to the final and saw Adrian's green and gold banner flutter in the breeze.

The hundred metres is only a matter of ten to twelve seconds, and she drew the outside lane, so that on account of staggering, she never even saw her opponents as the starter's gun sent her hurtling from her blocks like a javelin thrown by a master hand, unconscious of the sinewy form close on her heels like a black shadow pursuing a sunbeam. Inches from the tape the shadow eclipsed the sun.

A silver. As she stood on the rostrum and watched the coveted gold handed to Lola Smithson, whose dark face

was split by a white-toothed grin, Rosamund had to fight
a sinking heart. Lola's legend seemed to be only too true.
She glanced towards the stadium. Adrian was standing
up in his place, waving the coloured handkerchief. She
knew a similar thought must be in both their minds.
There was still the four hundred metres, her best distance. She must beat Lola in that!

The other members of the British team were jubilant.
They had not expected Rosamund Prescott, almost an
outsider, to do so well. There was much back-slapping,
hand-shaking and a rush of eager reporters. Rosamund
herself felt no elation; silver was no use to her when she
had set her heart upon winning the gold ... for Adrian.
She brushed aside the persistent pressmen.

'I didn't win,' was all she would say.

There was still the four hundred metres.

Adrian congratulated her, but his manner was distrait,
as if he were thinking of something else. Nor did he suggest taking her back to his hotel, as she had half hoped
he would, until she remembered the Delaneys were there.
A half hint that she would like to see something of the
country was met by the stern rejoinder that she had better
not waste energy she would need for her next race by
junketing about. This was the old Adrian, not the lover
she had begun to expect. He did not come again to the
Olympic Village; possibly he had been refused entrance,
but Rosamund was disappointed. Was it possible he
feared he had said too much on the previous day and was
anxious to avoid further indiscretions?

The British coach offered her advice for her next event.
She was certain to qualify in the heats and the semi-final,
even if she came up against Lola, and he hoped she
would draw her, for it would give her a better chance to
gauge her form before the final.

'She never lets up from the moment the gun goes,' he told her. 'Nor must you. Let her get ahead of you and you're lost.'

'This is Lola's second Olympic,' the team manager said. 'If Rosamund gets another silver she'll have performed a miracle.'

But not the miracle for which Adrian hoped.

Rosamund did not draw Lola in her heat. She won it, but learned that Lola had run hers in a faster time. Another silver was predicted for Rosamund Prescott, but, she thought feverishly, *it must be the gold.*

The semi-final was run in the afternoon, and Rosamund was drawn against Lola Smithson. Adrian's place in the stadium was vacant. Waiting for the start, Rosamund strained her eyes trying to distinguish him and a flutter of green and gold. It did not come, and as far as she could see he was not there. Anxiety gripped her. Could something have happened to him, or was he merely delayed? Surely it could not be, that believing she had no chance against Lola, he had not bothered to come? He must know how much she relied upon his presence to encourage and sustain her? It was his will, more than her own, that drove her forward and he could not fail her.

'On your marks. Set!'

Still no lean brown hand waving the emblazoned handkerchief.

The gun went.

Rosamund came in third behind Lola and Anna Cornish, the Canadian.

'Anything wrong?' the coach demanded. 'Not feeling dickey, are you?'

'What's wrong?' echoed the reporters. 'You're being backed for second place.'

'Nothing is wrong,' she replied. 'I qualified, I'll be in the final.'

But everything was wrong because Adrian had not been there.

On her return to the village she was handed a note, and her heartbeat quickened as she recognised Adrian's sprawling writing. He must have been delayed or obstructed and this was to tell her that he would be at the final without fail. She tore it open and read:

'Dear Ros,

Just a hurried line to tell you how sorry I am that I can't stay to watch you win. Dr Delaney has suddenly been recalled. You know how it is with doctors and this is an emergency only he can deal with. He wants me to go with him and for personal reasons which I'll explain later, it's imperative that I should. Please forgive me for deserting you, but I know you'll be all right. Believe me, I have a very strong inducement for going which at the moment I'd rather not disclose.

Yours.  A.B.

A very strong inducement! Of course, Madeleine would be returning with her father and had persuaded Adrian to accompany her. That he would certainly not want to disclose. He had watched her defeat by Lola, heard the record time in which she had won her four hundred metres heat and decided that Rosamund had no chance against her. So he had yielded to Madeleine's persuasions and gone without even coming to say goodbye to her, so sure was he that the miracle would not occur. But she was not defeated yet. There was still the final; if she ran as she had never run before she might still overcome the black shadow that dogged her, and prove Adrian's hasty assumption wrong. She lifted her head proudly. She would win. Then a wave of depression submerged her. It did not matter if she did or did not ... now. Hitherto she had been only dimly aware of Madeleine's presence in San Antonio. But she had been staying at the same hotel with Adrian, seeing him every day, accompanying him upon various expeditions when he was not at the stadium, dining and talking with him in the evenings.

She had had endless opportunities to exert her influence upon Adrian, and Rosamund did not doubt that it was upon her account that Adrian had decided to return with her and her father to France. Madeleine was not interested enough in athletics to stay on in San Antonio without her father, though she might have done if Adrian had proved obdurate, but he had fallen in with her wishes. For personal reasons, Adrian had written. His explanation would be that they had at last become engaged.

As for that interlude in the canteen, it meant nothing. He had been excited by the Olympic atmosphere, had envisioned her bedecked with golden medals, perhaps had meant to spur her on to greater effort with the bribe of a Caribbean holiday, but when he saw her chances receding he had turned to Madeleine again, yielded to her importunities and abandoned Rosamund.

Yet she could not convince herself that he would act so meanly, unpredictable though he was. He might be regretting what he had said to her, but surely he was not such a cad as to take refuge in flight?

But whatever had motivated him, the fact remained, he had gone.

It seemed her colleagues were better informed about

the Delaneys than she was, for when she went into the
dining room to try to eat some of the food she did not
want, the Canadian girl, Anna, came to her table.

'My, you sure pushed me this afternoon,' she said
wonderingly, 'and you almost unknown. By the next
Olympics you'll be a world champion and have broken
the world record.'

Anna had a pleasant open face and a frank manner.
Her candid brown eyes surveyed the other girl admir-
ingly.

Rosamund smiled wanly. 'Nice of you to say so, but a
lot can happen in four years.'

She would never run in another Olympiad.

'Oh, I don't know, time flies awfully fast,' Anna remarked tritely, sitting down opposite to Rosamund. 'I
hear that fascinating coach of yours, the one who used to
wave to you, didn't wait for the finish. My people are
staying in the same hotel where he was with some French
folk. The girl was his fiancée, wasn't she? A very smart
chick, my brother said, but not really interested in the
games. He wasn't surprised when she upped and left,
though he thought *he* might have stayed, seeing that
you're one of his runners, but perhaps she wouldn't like
that. Engaged girls can be nearly as possessive as wives.'

'I suppose they can,' Rosamund agreed vaguely.

'That Doctor Delaney is quite a V.I.P.,' Anna went on.
'Got a big clinic in France where he's trying out some
new treatment for paralysis or some such. He was sent for
suddenly, and my brother overheard his daughter telling
Mr Belmont that she had to go too, and if he didn't come
with her he'd be missing an opportunity he'd regret all
his life.'

Madeleine's ultimatum, Rosamund thought drearily;

she had not been so complacent as Adrian seemed to imagine.

'What did he say to that?' she asked through stiff lips.

'He couldn't get away fast enough.' Something in Rosamund's face checked Anna's gossip. 'I say, you knew about him being engaged and all that, didn't you? I haven't put my big foot into something?'

'Of course I knew,' Rosamund declared bravely, but mendaciously. 'Mademoiselle Delaney has a much stronger claim on him than I have, and he was quite right to go if she needed him. I don't require any more advice at this stage, and if I do, there's always the official team coach.'

Not to this friendly stranger would she give a hint of how her revelations had hurt her. Adrian's note had been ambiguous and could be interpreted in several ways, but there was nothing ambiguous about Anna's statements. Everyone at the hotel had recognised Madeleine as Adrian's fiancée and all he had said to her on the eve of her first heat had been nothing but pretty fantasy. She would have been the first to deny that he was a philanderer, but it would seem she had been wrong, and she was not the first girl to lose her heart to a charming rake.

Rosamund was not placed in the finals. She came in fourth and her time was 52.99 against Lola's 49.1, the slowest she had run in the Olympics.

She had to stay for the closing ceremonies and run the barrage of disappointed questioners. Why had she failed so dismally in the four hundred metres after such a promising start?

'Because I didn't run fast enough,' she retorted brusquely.

She was sick to death of the heat, the crowds and perpetual badgering. The real answer was that the man she loved had left her flat at the request of another woman, but that she could not put forward as an excuse, would not acknowledge it as one even to herself.

Adrian had treated her very badly and if he preferred Madeleine she was not going to whine; he deserved the French girl, who, she assured herself, would make his life a hell. He was welcome to go and burn in it.

# CHAPTER NINE

ROSAMUND went straight home after her return to England and waited anxiously for a communication from Adrian. None came, so that she was forced to conclude that since she had failed to win the coveted Olympic gold he had lost interest in her. When she rang up Mrs Grey at Belmont to enquire about his whereabouts, Adela told her he was in France on a long and indefinite stay with the Delaneys. She put her own interpretation upon that.

'Mark my words,' she announced portentously, 'he'll come back a married man.'

'But you expected to be asked to the wedding,' Rosamund reminded her, aware of a dead, empty feeling permeating her whole being.

Mrs Grey's sigh was audible over the wire. 'Maybe I'm not good enough for Miss Delaney,' she said. 'Daresay I'd look a bit out of place among all her smart French friends. Not that the Master'd care, but it's the bride has the say-so in these affairs. When are you coming back, Miss Rosamund?'

Rosamund told her that she was taking a short holiday after the Games and she would let the housekeeper know when she was returning. In actual fact she did not mean to return at all. She would have to go down to Belmont to collect her belongings and to give Mrs Grey formal notice in Adrian's absence, and she recalled with a stab of anguish his invitation in San Antonio to go away with him to some tropic isle to escape the winter chill. For the hundredth time she wondered what had induced him to propose such a fantasy unless it was the glamour of the gold medal which she had not won. My Golden Girl, he had called her, not foreseeing that she would only be a silver one. He had not even waited to learn the outcome of the four hundred metres, but had rushed away at Madeleine's instigation. He would have heard of her defeat soon enough, and since the miracle had not happened, he had dropped her.

That was the hard fact which she had to accept, and there was no point in dwelling upon dreams that had not materialised. She had to decide what she was going to do about her future, since Adrian had made no practical plans for it. The position at Belmont had only been an excuse to finance her while she was training, and would presumably terminate now Adrian was no longer coaching her, and she certainly did not want to be there when he returned engaged or married to Madeleine Delaney. Nor did she suppose that he had any further interest in her career. Meanwhile there were press interviews, television appearances and future fixtures being offered to her in bewildering succession—bewildering, because formerly Adrian had managed all her business and her father proved to be a poor substitute. Without the stimulation and inspiration of Adrian's presence, she lost all heart and decided to make an end, by retiring. She horrified her father by refusing to make any appearances and turned down all offers, including an invitation to join a British team going out to Los Angeles.

'I'm giving up,' she told him. 'I'll never run again.'

Mr Prescott took the view that his daughter was overstrained and hoped that her ambition would revive when she was rested, and so he told the reporters who sought to interview her, but he was perturbed when she ceased to do any more training.

'You'll lose form and fitness,' he warned her.

'It doesn't matter. Dad, I meant it when I said I was giving up.'

If Adrian had written, if he had expressed a wish that she should set her sights on any of the major events of next season, she might have retracted, but he gave no sign. Having decided to marry Madeleine, for so she concluded, he thought it was wiser to sever all connection with her. He could have done it more gently, she thought sadly, but he never had given much consideration to her personal feelings, and after his lapse in San Antonio, he probably did not know what to say to her.

Eventually she went down to Belmont, and found Mrs Grey also had had no communication from her errant employer.

'Don't worry,' the housekeeper said complacently. 'He's probably too busy courting, he's no call to bother about the estate or the house, he has an efficient manager to run the former and me to look after the latter. It isn't the first time he's taken himself off for a month or two without contacting us. If anything happened to him his solicitor would inform us, but he hates being tied. He wrote to me when he arrived in France telling me he'd be away for some time.'

'Didn't he give you any instructions about me?' Rosamund asked. Adrian seemed to have overlooked her altogether.

'He didn't mention you. I suppose he thought you'd go on training on your own, but if you're giving up and want to get another job, I can accept your notice in his absence, I'm responsible for the staff, but Lucie and I'll be sorry to lose you.'

'I don't feel I'm needed here,' Rosamund pointed out.

'And now I've given up running there's no point in staying.'

Mrs Grey agreed and remarked with unintentional cruelty that it might be a good thing if she did go before the new Mrs Belmont arrived.

'For I couldn't help noticing she rather resented your presence here,' she observed. 'It was only natural, you're so pretty, and the Master did make rather a pet of you.'

Rosamund flinched, and said a little bitterly:

'Just like a puppy, disciplined one moment, petted the next. Well, I failed to fulfil his expectations, so I'll take myself off.'

Mrs Grey looked at her wonderingly.

'But you won a silver medal, Miss Rosamund, it was in all the papers. Wasn't the Master pleased about that?'

'No, it wasn't what he wanted,' Rosamund said shortly.

She took an affectionate farewell of Lucie, promising that the child should come and visit her some Sunday, but with her new preoccupation with school, she knew Lucie would soon forget her.

Before she left, Rosamund went on a pilgrimage accompanied by the two dogs round the sports complex and the park beyond. She was saying goodbye to Belmont and all that had happened there. She stood for a few moments by the spot under the wall where she had jumped down on that memorable day and recalled Adrian's comment:

'I knew you meant trouble, and so you did.'

The meeting had meant trouble for her too—worse than trouble, heartbreak. She turned away with a sigh, firmly dismissing the black-haired ghost that seemed to linger in the shadow of the trees, leaning upon his stick and watching her with inscrutable blue eyes.

Rosamund obtained a job in the sports department of

a well-known store. She was offered a high salary for the use of her name to promote a brand of sports shoes and her autograph if she were asked for it. She would rather have been anonymous, but as her father said, she might as well make what she could out of her career, and she would all too soon be forgotten. With employment in short supply and having been out of the market for two years, she could not afford to be choosey.

The autumn days sped by, and then to her surprise she received a phone call from Tony Bridges.

He rang up one evening to ask if she would care to go to a dinner dance given by a sports association for all the notable athletes of the year. He had a spare ticket as his date had let him down.

'I know it sounds a bit of a backhanded invitation,' he said apologetically, 'but it seems a pity to waste the ticket and I thought you might possibly be free and would like to go. It's time we got together again.'

About to refuse, Rosamund wavered. It would be good to see Tony and hear his news; they had always been friends, and it was foolish to continue to mope over Adrian's desertion. She must take up her life again, make more social contacts in an endeavour to forget what might have been, and Tony was just the person to help her to do so.

She bought a new dress for the occasion, a long one in grey and shell pink chiffon with a filmy grey drapery over her shoulders in place of sleeves. She wore silver slippers and a silver ornament in her hair. She was rewarded by the appreciation in Tony's glance when he beheld her.

'You look lovely, Ros. It's a long time no see, and I don't know why I've neglected you so long.'

'We've both been otherwise engaged,' she suggested as

he handed her into the taxi he had hired to collect her in preference to facing the parking problem with his car.

'I haven't congratulated you yet,' he said as he settled down beside her. 'Pity, though, that you didn't get the gold.'

'Please forget what I didn't do and remember what I did,' she said tartly. Then, sensing his hurt surprise: 'Sorry, Tony, but if only you knew how many people have made that remark!'

'It's because it was such a near thing,' he explained. 'Pipped at the tape. Too bad.'

Just how bad he could not know.

She hastened to tell him about her new occupation, and to her relief he did not refer to Adrian or Belmont. As usual he was full of his own concerns and was hoping to be selected for the World Cup team next season.

'You will be, as a matter of course?' he queried enviously.

'I've given up athletics,' she returned.

'Have you indeed? Oh well, most girls don't take them very seriously. I suppose you've other things on your mind? Got engaged yet?'

She told him she was unattached.

'Then why give up running?'

'It took too much time. I'm concentrating upon earning a living.'

'Which you couldn't do at Belmont, and of course if the great man was coaching you, he'd veto romance, didn't think it mixed well with sport, but now you're free of him you can look around. Wouldn't like to take up with me again, would you?'

She laughed. 'We were never serious, Tony, and what about the girl whose ticket I'm using? Isn't she the current flame?'

'She's not a patch on you for looks,' Tony told her, 'but she's rather more forthcoming. I'm afraid she *is* getting serious.'

'Even though she stood you up tonight?'

'Yes . . . well, we had a bit of a disagreement, but she'll come round. She can't do without me,' he declared complacently.

They had reached their destination, and as she alighted from the taxi, Rosamund reflected that she was a long way from finding Tony indispensable, but his admiration had boosted her wounded ego.

They danced together for the remainder of the evening after the somewhat formal dinner. Noticing the admiring glances from other men that Rosamund was earning, Tony returned to the attack.

'I'm not all that gone on Joanna,' he declared, 'and after all, you were the first in the field. Couldn't we start again, Ros? I believe I could become serious about you.'

She shook her head, smiling. 'Best stick to your Joanna, Tony. I've decided to become an old maid.'

'Rubbish, you aren't spinster material, darling.' His hold tightened jealously, and his hazel eyes became amorous. 'It's Belmont, isn't it? Women all fall for him in spite of his nasty temper and his groggy knee. But you know it's no use hoping for anything from him.'

'I never did, and he's in France getting married to the girl he's always been contracted to,' Rosamund said flatly.

'Poor kid!' Tony lightly kissed her hair and laid his cheek against hers, having divined rather more than Rosamund wanted him to know. At that moment the press photographer who was prowling round the room snapped them.

'Please, Tony,' Rosamund pleaded, 'don't let's talk

about Mr Belmont. As I've given up running he's no longer coaching me and we're unlikely to meet again.'

'Good show,' Tony approved heartlessly. 'So now we can start again.'

But she refused to commit herself, insisting that he would be wiser to make it up with Joanna.

The photograph appeared in the popular press with the caption:

'Is Britain's silver medallist engaged to athlete Tony Bridges?' followed by a brief résumé of their respective careers.

Mr Prescott showed the picture to his daughter.

'May I ask the same question?' he asked, grinning.

'Of course we're not engaged. You know celebrities are wide open to that sort of nonsense. I only went to a dance with Tony.'

Her father looked at her thoughtfully.

'You were thick enough at one time, and he's a nice boy. A bit unstable, but you'd supply the incentive he needs. You could do a lot worse, Ros.'

'I know I could, but I don't want him.' She looked at the photograph. Her eyes were closed in her upturned face, and Tony's was buried in her hair, while their bodies were pressed together. They might well have been in the throes of amorous ecstasy, thus could the camera lie. 'Pity we were caught at the wrong moment,' she observed. 'Later on I told him he was wasting his time.'

She knew such speculations were often made about people in the limelight, but soon, very soon now, her name would be forgotten and she would be lost in the obscurity of a department store. The running track had become a thing of the past.

To finalise her break with her old life, she made a parcel of the topaz necklace and her silver medal and sent it by registered post addressed to Adrian at Belmont House.

The winter passed, and to Mr Prescott's disappointment, Rosamund's ambition did not return with the spring.

'You've really given up, Ros?' he asked her.

She assured him that she had.

Christmas had come and gone bringing a flood of memories and cards from Mrs Grey and Lucie, but nothing from Adrian. Nor was there any announcement of his marriage. From Lucie, who came to spend the promised Sunday with the Prescotts, Rosamund ascertained that he was still abroad.

'Winter sports,' Lucie suggested.

Rosamund recalled that Madeleine had had some aspirations in that direction, but Adrian had said it was a long time ago. Perhaps, under his direction, they had been revived. After all, there were gold medals to be won at the Winter Olympics as well.

He has to have someone to bully and cajole to win the honours he can't win himself, Rosamund thought bitterly.

Then one bright spring morning he walked into Rosamund's department at the store.

A teenage girl sat on the chair provided while Rosamund fitted her with a pair of sports shoes. She was on her knees, tying the laces of a white canvas shoe trimmed with red and blue, when looking up she caught sight of a proud patrician head bent over a glass case containing mugs and plates decorated with pheasants, grouse and other game birds. Her heart seemed to stop, and she became rigid, staring.

'I'd prefer black and yellow ones,' the girl was saying. She glanced at Rosamund's fixed face and exclaimed impatiently: 'Hey, miss, not gone into a trance, have you? I'd like to see some black and yellow shoes.'

'I'm sorry.' Rosamund removed the rejected ones and went to the stack of boxes behind her counter. Between them hung a mirror reflecting the showroom. Could it really be Adrian? She stared at his reflection. Face and form were identical with the man she had known and loved, but he carried no stick and as he spoke to an assistant and walked with-him across the floor to look at some cricket bats, he moved with a long graceful stride without trace of a limp. That indicated that he could not be Adrian Belmont, but he was so like him that she had been thrown into confusion.

Hastily she selected what was required and returned to her customer, resolutely ignoring the two distant figures, the assistant and Adrian's double.

The girl's needs finally satisfied, Rosamund wrote out the bill, saying mechanically: 'Pay at the desk. Good morning, madam,' and proceeded to put away the unwanted boxes behind the counter. Turning round, she met over its glossy breadth the brilliant azure gaze and satirical smile that she knew so well, and she clutched at the edge of the counter for support.

'Well, well, well!' he drawled. 'So you've become an efficient saleswoman, Miss Prescott, though you once told me you had no aptitude for selling.' He picked up a pair of running shoes displayed on the counter which bore a facsimile of her signature and studied them with ironical amusement. 'So you're cashing in on your athletic achievements. What did they pay you for that?' He indicated the writing. 'And aren't I entitled to a commission?'

The assistant who had been attending to him came hurrying up.

'We have a further selection of bats over there, sir,' he indicated the spot. 'If you will step this way, sir.'

'I'm installing a cricket pitch at Belmont,' Adrian told Rosamund, ignoring him. 'We're getting up a village team. So good for the young people, don't you think?'

Rosamund could not speak. Adrian's unexpected appearance had unnerved her. Dumbly she stared at her hands clutching the counter edge and his eyes followed hers, noting her ringless fingers.

'Not married yet?' he asked carelessly.

With an effort she regained the use of her tongue, suppressing the rising tide of emotion his presence had caused. Copying his tone, she queried lightly:

'Should I be?'

'Signs and portents indicated yes.'

'I might ask you the same question,' she retorted.

A shadow crossed his face. 'My prospective bride walked out on me,' he said shortly, and turned to the curious-eyed assistant. 'Where are these bats?'

They moved away and Rosamund watched them in bewilderment. What could Adrian mean? That Madeleine had jilted him? That seemed to be highly improbable, and why did he suppose that she should be married? Who to? Suddenly she recalled the photograph taken at the dance of herself and Tony. Adrian must have seen it and drawn his own conclusions, but surely he could not believe it meant anything, and there had been no follow-up announcement of an engagement. In a daze she watched him moving about the floor in consultation with the assistant; he was buying a complete cricket outfit, balls, wickets, the lot ... for the villagers at Belmont who hitherto he had barred from his premises. Not only was he back at Belmont, but he seemed to have had a change of heart ... and what had happened to Madeleine? Surely she would not approve of such violation of her privacy, or had she accepted the role of Lady Bountiful? That did not seem in character either, and Adrian had stated that she had walked out on him. One thing was very apparent: Adrian's limp was cured.

Rosamund had never heard exactly what had caused it. Mrs Grey had mentioned vaguely a shattered patella, a severed tendon and a permanent injury to cartilages and muscles. But modern surgery could perform wonders with grafts and replacements, so something of the sort must have been done to Adrian.

His order given, the Master of Belmont arranged for the despatch of the goods to his home. The transaction completed, he moved towards the escalator to the ground floor with the new easy stride he had acquired. He was going without a further word to Rosamund, leaving all her queries unanswered. Desperately she ran to intercept him, and reached him as he was about to step on to the moving stairway.

'Adrian!' she cried.

He turned about. 'You wish to speak to me, Miss Prescott?'

His cold formality struck her like a blow, but she refused to be intimidated.

'Your knee,' she whispered. 'It's cured.'

He smiled crookedly.

'Dr Delaney performed the miracle.'

Rosamund drew a long breath. So that was what he had meant when he had talked about miracles! He had always been abnormally sensitive about his limp and had hinted that his incapacity was responsible for his celibacy, while she had thought ... dimly she began to perceive there had been a terrible misunderstanding. She said faintly:

'Is that why you left San Antonio so suddenly?'

'Of course. It had to be something of the utmost importance to cause me to go. You should have realised that.' His eyes, cold as blue ice, pierced her like a knife. 'But you couldn't wait to learn the outcome.'

'But I didn't know ... you never wrote ... never explained.'

'I left with Dr Delaney, an osteopath, wasn't that significant? I was unable to write because after the operation I got some sort of infection. When I was well enough to take notice again I was told you'd given up running and were engaged to Tony Bridges. I was shown a picture that seemed to prove it. Congratulations, Ros, I don't blame you. You always did have a yen for that young layabout.'

'He's not a layabout!' Mechanically she defended Tony, while she strove to assimilate what Adrian had told her. Someone had deliberately shown him that unfortunate picture and had sought to mislead him. Madeleine most likely, though he had not mentioned her name.

'Miss Prescott.' The floor manager had come up to them. 'You've left your counter unattended, and it is not permitted to entertain friends in the firm's time.'

Adrian gave the suave well-tailored figure a look of dislike.

'Miss Prescott came to remind me that I needed a pair of running shoes,' he said blandly, and began to retrace his steps.

'But these are ladies' shoes,' the manager objected as they reached Rosamund's counter.

'I require them for a lady.' Adrian picked up the same pair that he had been examining previously. 'The Prescott line,' he observed. 'They didn't name a shoe for me, but I could hardly expect anything so inappropriate with my dot-and-carry-one gait as it was then.'

Some of the old bitterness sounded in his voice, and the manager looked at him as if he suspected he was a harmless lunatic.

'Are those the right size?' he asked stiffly.

'Oh, they'll do. I only want them as a souvenir,' Adrian told him. 'But this is Miss Prescott's domain, isn't it? We won't detain you.'

The man seemed about to protest, changed his mind and shrugged his shoulders.

'Attend to the gentleman,' he said to Rosamund, and marched off.

'Do you really want these shoes?' Rosamund asked diffidently.

'Certainly. They'll please Lucie. We'll hang them up beside your silver medal. Why did you discard that, Ros? It was an achievement.'

'Not when you wanted the gold,' she murmured, mechanically parcelling the shoes.

'You did your best, but you also returned my poor gift.'

'I couldn't keep it when ... when ...'

'You'd changed your mind?'

'It wasn't that.' How could she explain under the watchful eye of the distant manager, without time to absorb the significance of Adrian's revelations and her ignorance of what had transpired between him and Madeleine? He studied her, frowning, as she made out the bill, and then shrugged his shoulders.

'Don't look so woebegone,' he chided her. 'Surely you can't be already regretting your ... choice. Or perhaps you're regretting Belmont. Madeau did say, though I didn't believe her ...' He broke off as if he had suddenly become aware of the black looks the manager was throwing in their direction. 'I'd best be off before I'm again accused of distracting you from your duties, and I don't want to buy any more shoes. Good day, Miss Prescott.'

He took the bill and the parcel and walked away without looking back.

Madeau said ... what had Madeleine said? Rosamund was sure that it was she who had shown Adrian that photograph. Recalling her spiteful innuendoes, she must also have been responsible for his remark about regretting Belmont, though he had qualified it by indicating that he did not believe Rosamund was mercenary. Still, the doubt had been sown or he would not have mentioned it. She had learned, much too late, that the French girl had not been the reason for his sudden departure. Possibly vacancies in Dr Delaney's clinic were few and far between and that was why when one had occurred, Madeleine had insisted that he must not miss the opportunity, but why, oh, why had he not told her where he was going and with what object? She would have understood, she would not then have been so devastated, she might even have won her race.

The answer was Adrian's absurd sensitivity about his disablement. He had not told her in case the operation was a failure. He had said he would take her away if the miracle had occurred, but if he had remained lame, he would have repudiated her. It was all so ridiculous because, loving him as she did, his disability meant nothing to her at all, but it did to him. He did not consider he was a whole man while he limped. It was his arrogant pride that lay between them. It had shown several times in his jealousy of Tony, because Tony was still an athlete, and Adrian had felt inferior to him.

All that Rosamund could understand, though she

thought Adrian had behaved foolishly, but what had happened since? Was it possible that when the operation was successful, Adrian had said he was returning to her and Madeleine had intervened, fearing her own hopes were about to be dashed? It was more than possible, it was probable. The photograph in the paper had given her a weapon to prove that Rosamund was fickle, that with Adrian out of the way she had returned to her old love, and that what had attracted her to the Master of Belmont was his possessions. With Adrian enduring a slow convalescence in her father's clinic she would have had ample opportunity to instil her poison.

Whatever had occurred, she had managed to turn Adrian against his former protégée, that was obvious in the way he had looked and spoken to her today. Yet he had been chivalrous enough to buy a pair of shoes he did not want to save her from a reprimand when she had left her post to try to delay him. But did he still care? Had he consoled himself with Madeleine after all? Were they engaged, and was she at Belmont? He had said his bride had walked out on him, and he might have been referring to herself. The thought was bitter-sweet, but wounded pride might drive him into Madeleine's arms, had perhaps already done so.

Rosamund was in a turmoil of uncertainty. Somehow she must discover what had happened, for if there was the slightest chance of clearing up the misunderstanding and refuting Madeleine's misrepresentations, she must take it. She dared not hope that Adrian would become reconciled to her. Too long a time had elapsed between that enchanted hour at San Antonio and the dreary present, and she had given up the athletics that had been a bond between them. But she was determined that he should learn the truth, that she had not been flirting with

Tony while he had been ill, and she had never had any designs upon his property. At the expense of her own pride, she would make any sacrifice to convince him that he had cruelly misjudged her.

She considered telephoning. If Adela took her call, she could tell her if Madeleine was in England, but that made no difference to her resolution. If Adrian did, it would not be satisfactory. The telephone was not the best medium to attempt clarification. The other person's face could not be seen, interruptions could occur, and he might even cut her off before she had said all she wanted to say. Letters could be mislaid or intercepted, and she was not good at expressing herself on paper. No, the obvious course to pursue was to go down to Belmont and find out for herself what was happening, and if possible meet Adrian face to face. She could always say she had come to see Lucie, who would welcome a visit from her, if she needed an excuse. Moreover, she would probably learn more about what was vital to her if she took the household by surprise.

Rosamund was unable to carry out her plan immediately, for her mother went down with influenza and she had to spend all her spare time nursing her. Because of her employment, she could only go at a weekend, and a fortnight passed before she could get away. During that time she half hoped to receive some word from Adrian, but naturally none came. He had written her off and would not dream of contacting her.

At last, on a really beautiful Saturday morning in early May, with Mrs Prescott no longer an invalid, Rosamund was able to set forth upon her fateful journey to Belmont.

## CHAPTER TEN

MAY, when it is sunny and warm, as it more often is not, is the fairest month of the year, with the trees in new leaf and all the blossom flowering. In the country the hedges are covered with the white froth of the hawthorn and in the woodlands bluebells spread a carpet. Lilacs raise mauve cones in cottage gardens and laburnums drip golden fountains from feathery foliage.

Rosamund, wearing wide-legged trousers, a tee-shirt and a suede jacket, travelled in a crowded bus with only a limited view of the countryside from an inside seat. She sighed with relief when she reached her destination and could enjoy the sights and scents of late spring as she walked up to Belmont. She did not anticipate having any trouble with the lodgekeeper; he knew her now, and she would say she had come to visit Mrs Grey and Lucie. It was of her first excursion to the place that she was thinking as she trudged along. What a lot had happened during the intervening two years, and how unwittingly she had rushed upon her fate when she had climbed the park wall. The animosity she had felt then towards Belmont's master had changed to unrequited love, that might be considered a misfortune, but she did not regret it. Knowing and loving Adrian had enriched her life and she yearned to see him again. But would he listen to her or would he refuse to speak to her? Perhaps she had been foolish to come, for he had probably lost all interest in the affairs of Miss Rosamund Prescott. He might not be at home, and that would be a reprieve, for she was beginning to repent of her impulsive action in coming here. But having come so far, she would not turn back until she had at least seen Mrs Grey.

When she reached the wrought iron gates she saw to her surprise that they were wide open, and parked just inside were several motor coaches. Walking through them, she stopped to read a notice fastened to the gate, which was inscribed: 'The Belmont Recreational Centre'. This was an innovation Adrian had not mentioned; he had only told her he was inaugurating a cricket team. Rosamund continued her way up between the lime trees among which bees buzzed in their search for nectar among the small green flowers that filled the air with sweetness. Adrian seemed to have widened his scope considerably. From coaching a team of young men whom he deemed it necessary to protect from over-enterprising young women, he had made his resources available to all the countryside. Cricket matches were in progress on either side of her; girls and youths were running and hurdling, and families were picnicking among the trees. She reflected that among such an influx of strangers, nobody would notice her.

Rosamund rounded the curve that concealed the house and now she could see the distant sports complex. A bicycle race was now in progress on the track and excited shouts came from the swimming pool. The house itself looked as usual, its front door set ajar to admit the sunshine; the invaders kept to a respectful distance away from it and it looked deserted. As she reached the last tree before the gravel sweep in front of it, a car slid past her and drew up in front of the entrance steps. Rosamund halted in the shade of the tree and watched as a tall, thin man descended from the driver's seat. He was joined by his woman passenger, and her heart sank as she recognised Madeleine Delaney.

A figure in white flannels came running up from the cricket pitch accompanied by two red dogs. Adrian had spied his visitors and had come to welcome them. He moved with a swift, agile grace that replaced the familiar limp. In all the time she had known him Rosamund had never seen him run, and she realised the enormous debt he owed to Dr Delaney, a debt the doctor might expect him to discharge by marrying his daughter. The doctor greeted him French fashion with an embrace and a kiss upon either cheek. Adrian endured the ordeal and then turned to Madeleine, according her the same treatment, which she received with a little affected laugh and obvious gratification. To the watching Rosamund they appeared a happy family party.

Dr Delaney seemed to be remonstrating with Adrian, probably chiding him for doing too much, for he indicated his leg with an expressive gesture. Madeleine's high, shrill voice reached Rosamund beneath her tree.

'Papa had to attend a conference in London and I told him we must come and see how you were progressing. You are never long out of our thoughts, *mon ami*, and Papa fears you run too much, for the knee is not yet strong. But what goes on here? A village *fête*?'

Even over the distance between them Rosamund could see her disdainful look. Adrian's reply was inaudible and she moved round the bole of the tree to conceal herself from his view. It was ill luck that her visit had coincided with one from the Delaneys, and it was apparent that they were not staying in the house, nor had they been expected. But Adrian had rushed to greet them and had received them with affection, which indicated obviously the way things were going. She, Rosamund, was an outsider, a trespasser, and Adrian would not welcome her appearance. She belonged to a past which he had turned his back upon together with the years of incapacity. He was a new man creating a new life with the help of the Delaneys and Rosamund had no part in it. She had better retreat before she was seen. She abandoned her intention of visiting Adela, who would be busy preparing tea for the visitors and might find her appearance an embarrassment. Though contrary to her prediction Adrian had returned from France unwed, there was every indication that he would not be so for long, and Mrs Grey would be correspondingly jubilant.

Rosamund turned away preparing to retrace her steps, hoping no one would observe her, but she had forgotten the dogs. As she moved, their keen sight recognised her figure and they were after her in a flash. Her scent confirming their eyesight, they bounded around her uttering sharp ecstatic barks. The canine heart knows no subterfuges. They had found an old friend who recalled memories of delightful races across the parkland. They were hoping she would run with them now.

'Down, Roland! Down, Oliver!' she sought to curb their enthusiasm, aware that the trio by the car were looking towards her.

'Go back to Master!' she urged, wanting to make her retreat before Adrian came to fetch them. Whether he had recognised her she could not tell, but the dogs' greeting was a giveaway, they would be suspicious of a stranger. However, Adrian was detained by Madeleine, who had her hand upon his arm and was speaking urgently, drawing him towards the open front door. She had guessed who the slight girlish figure was, and was anxious to prevent a meeting.

On sudden impulse, Rosamund turned aside and ran

swiftly into the crowd of villagers watching the cricket match. She would be less conspicuous among them than walking down the drive alone, and she might find an opportunity to conceal herself somewhere in the park. Adrian's whistle had recalled the dogs, who had unwillingly gone back to him.

In her haste and confusion Rosamund blundered on to the cricket pitch and a swipe from the batsman caught her full on her knee, so that her legs gave way and she collapsed ignominiously on the green, amidst loud recriminations from the players, the mildest being: 'Why can't you look where you're going?'

Red-faced, Rosamund scrambled to her feet and began to limp towards the shelter of the onlookers uttering vague apologies.

'You're hurt?' It was Adrian's voice, and he must have witnessed the stupid incident. Shamefaced, she mumbled that it was nothing much, while he put an arm around her to support her. The close contact, the sense of his dearly loved presence beside her, unnerved her.

'Oh, Adrian . . .' she whimpered on a half sob.

'Oh, Ros!' he mimicked her. Then gently: 'Is it very painful?'

'Just a little.' Feeling she needed to explain why she was there, she went on: 'I just thought I'd like to look at the place again, but I didn't mean to barge into a cricket match.' She laughed forcedly. 'There seem to be innovations since my time.'

'Yes, I've made some changes. I felt all this was too much for one man. By creating a sports centre, I'm giving thanks for my recovery.'

'A wonderful gesture,' she said enthusiastically, and then realised that he was leading her towards the house.

'I'm all right now,' she declared hurriedly. 'And I

must be on my way—I've a bus to catch.'

'You're not all right. Cricket balls are hard and you'd better rest that knee before you attempt to walk to the village. History seems to be repeating itself, only last time it was your head. You must be accident-prone.'

She stopped, resisting the pressure of his arm.

'I don't want to intrude, you have visitors.'

'Only the Delaneys. The doctor can look at your knee. As I think you know, he's an expert on joints.'

Still she hung back. 'I couldn't trouble him.'

'Don't be silly, Ros,' he reproved her severely. 'Or is the hospitality of my house obnoxious to you?'

'Oh, no, no!' she cried distressfully.

'Well then, come on.'

Perforce she had to yield. His solicitude was balm to her, but Madeleine would be at the house and she did not want to meet her. She began to protest again, but all he said was: 'Shut up.'

'You always did insist upon having your own way,' she complained.

'You never did know what was good for you,' he retorted. Then in a changed voice: 'Were you coming to see me?'

'Of course not,' she declared emphatically, and he gave her a bleak look. Not now would she admit that such had been her intention.

He took her into the drawing room through the french window, and put her into one of the big easy chairs. 'Better roll your trouser leg up so that we can assess the damage,' he suggested. 'Or shall I do it for you?'

He stood before her regarding her half-humorously, but she could not sense his mood. Was he resenting her presence? In reply to his question, she said hurriedly: 'Oh no, please!'

Luckily she was not wearing tights, only socks, and she gingerly rolled the wide flared leg of her trousers up above her knee. It was swelled but not yet discoloured, and she could flex the joint, though the movement was painful.

'I don't think it's more than bruised,' Adrian decided, 'but since he's here we'll ask the expert's opinion.'

Dr Delaney had dark eyes similar to his daughter's, but with a much kinder expression. He had a lean, clever face with a big nose. His skilful hands explored Rosamund's knee and confirmed Adrian's diagnosis.

'I have liniment that will relieve it,' he said gently. 'You are the lady who runs, *n'est-ce pas*? I fear you will not run for some weeks, but then the knee will be as good as before.'

'I've given up running,' Rosamund told him, and he looked surprised. 'I'm sorry to trouble you over such a trifle, but Mr Belmont insisted.'

'He is fearful of injury to knees,' Dr Delaney declared, smiling. 'But I do on him what you say ... the good job.' He glanced at Adrian, who was watching them with a satirical smile, and went on: 'I was disappointed that I could not wait for your race, *mademoiselle*. I was suddenly recalled to France.' He opened the bag beside him and took out a tube of salve. 'I always carry the first aid with me, and you see how wise I am. *Eh bien*, I have recently done experiments on injuries similar to Monsieur Belmont's with complete success, so we arrange he will return with me after the Games, but when I have to go so quick I ask him to come with me so that we can fit in the operation when most convenient to me.' He began to spread the salve over her knee.

'That was understandable,' Rosamund said, 'and as I failed to win the race, you didn't miss anything.'

'But *did* you understand?' Adrian enquired.

'Well, I do now, though your note was a bit vague,' she told him reproachfully, recalling all the unnecessary anguish she had suffered.

'Was it?' Adrian knitted his brows, trying to recall what he had said. 'I scribbled it in haste, but I was dead scared of raising false hopes. I'd told you I hoped for a miracle and was sure you'd know what the important matter was.'

She had completely misunderstood him.

'Well, it's all over now,' she said stonily.

He gave her a quizzical look. 'That's obvious.'

With deft fingers the doctor bandaged her knee and rolled down her trouser leg. Rosamund tried to stand up.

'*Non*,' he commanded, pushing her back into the depths of the chair. '*Restez là.*'

'But I can't ...'

'You can and you will,' Adrian insisted forcibly. 'After tea we'll see about driving you home.' He placed a footstool under her foot. 'As my friend says, rest it for now.'

Rosamund bit her lip with vexation. The last thing she wanted to do was to stay at Belmont, but she was literally tied by the leg. She would have to submit with good grace.

Adrian said with a wicked gleam in his eyes : 'Mademoiselle has a very jealous swain and she's afraid he won't understand.'

'Swain? *Comment?*'

Adrian waved a hand in vague explanation. 'Boyfriend—*un amant*.'

'*Eh bien*, physical wellbeing comes before affairs of the heart,' the doctor proclaimed. 'The *amant* must understand that.'

'Tony is not my lover,' Rosamund declared, two bright

spots of colour in her cheeks. She had come to Belmont to rid Adrian of that misconception, but she had not anticipated having to do so in front of a stranger. She looked at him appealingly, hoping that he would believe her. He was watching her with an enigmatical expression and as he met her eyes a malicious gleam came into his, and her heart sank. It no longer mattered to him what she felt about Tony, if indeed it ever had. She might as well have held her tongue.

Dr Delaney looked at his hands.

'If you will show me where I can wash, *mon garçon*.'

'Certainly. Come along.'

The two men went out of the room leaving Rosamund to her thoughts. Could she escape while they were absent? But her knee was stiff and painful and it was a long trek to the bus stop. While she hesitated, the door opened again and Madeleine came in.

She was wearing a trouser suit which bore the stamp of a Paris couturier. It comprised dark red trousers and tunic; the jacket she had been wearing when she arrived she had left in the car. Make-up and hair-do were immaculate, causing Rosamund to become conscious of her own dishevelled appearance. Her hair was tangled and bits of grass clung to her jacket, the result of her fall.

'So you are here again, *mademoiselle*,' Madeleine said insolently. 'Why can't you leave Mr Belmont alone?'

'This is the first time I've seen him for months,' Rosamund told her, 'except for a chance visit to my store, when he seemed to be under some sort of misapprehension, which I wish to clear up. That is why I came here today.'

'A wasted journey,' Madeleine stated scornfully. 'Mr Belmont takes no further interest in your doings since you failed to win the gold medal.' Rosamund winced visibly. 'It is immaterial to him whether there has been a misunderstanding or not, there probably has not—he sees through you, Miss Prescott, and your latest method of drawing attention to yourself was ill-judged. Running into the middle of a cricket match was the act of a lunatic.'

'It was a genuine accident,' Rosamund cried vehemently.

'*Ah, ma foi, allez conter celà à d'autres,*' Madeleine retorted, being the equivalent of 'tell it to the marines'. 'Did you expect to gain his sympathy by getting a crack on the knee? He considers you a nuisance. He abandoned you in San Antonio because he found you embarrassing. You would not understand that he was only coaching you out of the goodness of his heart because he believed you had talent, but you did not fulfil his hopes and your obvious infatuation had become wearisome.'

Madeleine had left the door open behind her and her high, shrill voice would be audible to anyone in the passage outside. Rosamund hoped fervently that there was no one within earshot.

'That may be so,' she admitted quietly, though she could not make herself believe Adrian had found her wearisome during those magic moments in the Olympic Village when he had told her that if the miracle occurred he would take her away to a tropical island.

The miracle had happened, but it had not been what she had supposed, and thanks to Madeleine's intervention he had dropped her.

'It was you, wasn't it, who showed Adrian the picture in the paper of me and Tony,' she went on, 'and persuaded him I was engaged to him.'

Madeleine raised her plucked eyebrows. 'Aren't you?'

'No. I never was and I never will be. I went to one

dance with Tony when that photo was taken, and I only went because I needed some distraction since Adrian had discarded me. But it didn't work and I haven't seen Tony since. I wanted Adrian to know the truth of it.'

She knew it was useless trying to justify herself to the French girl, but she could not let her insults pass without defending herself, and she wondered if she would offer any excuse.

'He will not care one way or the other,' Madeleine declared, 'and will you please desist from calling him by his name. That is a privilege reserved for his real friends. *Naturellement*, I showed him that picture, it is well he should know how you conduct yourself when he is absent. This Tony is of your age and class, he is the obvious choice for you, and you only leave him when you think you have a chance to become the mistress of Belmont, as I pointed out to Mr Belmont. When you are disappointed you go back to your former *jeunne homme*. Mr Belmont quite understood.'

'You mean you deliberately sought to turn him against me,' Rosamund accused her. 'When he was ill and easily influenced. Oh, God, if only I'd known what was happening!'

'I suppose you would have come rushing over to France and thrusting yourself in where you were not wanted, like you've done today.'

Rosamund was becoming more and more convinced that Adrian had not abandoned her until Madeleine had worked upon him assisted by that unfortunate photograph, and what he had said at San Antonio had been genuine. When he had recovered he had not communicated with her because Madeleine had persuaded him she had gone back to Tony. Everything he had said since pointed to such a supposition. Circumstances had been against her and it was too late now to hope for a reconciliation. He had put her out of his life and was going to marry Madeleine out of gratitude to her father.

In reply to Madeleine's suggestion, she said steadily:

'I might have done just that, because I love Adrian, Miss Delaney, and I shall always love him in a way you'd never understand, and I'm not ashamed to confess it. Rich or poor, lame or sound, it makes no difference. I'm glad I came today and have met you, because I've learned he didn't leave San Antonio on your account, but because he had to take an opportunity which you yourself said he must not miss. You've admitted that it was your lies and spite that kept us apart. Well, it's all over now and I promise I'll not trouble either of you again once I've gone from here. Moreover, I wish you both every happiness.'

She turned away, covering her eyes with her hand, aware that her knee was aching, but it was much less than the pain in her heart.

She expected some sort of an outburst from Madeleine, and when none came, she uncovered her eyes and saw that Adrian had come in and was standing beside her looking at the French girl with anything but a pleasant expression.

'Quite frankly I've been eavesdropping,' he told her, 'and I found your remarks most illuminating, my dear Madeau. I couldn't bring myself to interrupt until all was revealed.' He shot Rosamund a lightning glance compounded of mischief and something she could not define. 'So, Madeau, all that sympathy you ladled out to me during my convalescence was designed to separate me from Ros. I might have known it!'

'I had to try and save you from your folly,' Madeleine declared. 'She . . .' she jerked her head towards

Rosamund, 'is not worthy of you or Belmont. A little jumped-up adventuress who . . .'

'That will do, Madeau,' he interrupted her. 'I know better than you do what Ros is.' He glanced towards her again and said softly. 'She has a heart of gold.'

Rosamund raised her head proudly as he moved towards her, knowing that he must have overheard her declaration of love, but as she had told Madeleine, she was not ashamed of it. As their eyes met she saw in his a flicker of blue flame; whatever Madeleine might say he was not indifferent to her.

But before he reached her, the rattle of the tea trolley interrupted whatever he was about to say—or do—and Mrs Grey pushed it into the room.

'Miss Rosamund!' she exclaimed, beaming. 'How lovely to see you, but you've been in the wars again, I'm told. Belmont doesn't seem to be very healthy for you.'

'That's unfortunate,' Adrian said, laughing. 'For that's where she's going to live in future.'

The Delaneys had gone. Tea had been constrained by Madeleine's glowering presence, which her father's affability had failed to counteract. He would have welcomed Adrian as a son-in-law, but he had known for some time that his affections were engaged elsewhere and had shrewdly suspected their object was the golden-haired girl who had run so gracefully at San Antonio. That there had been an impediment which had now been removed was obvious, and he beamed upon them paternally, to his daughter's disgust. Dusk was falling when they took their leave and Adrian said he must go and supervise the exodus of the villagers who were also departing. Rosamund limped into the back premises to see Lucie and receive Mrs Grey's congratulations.

'We've missed you,' the housekeeper said. 'So you're going to be mistress here? Well, I don't doubt we'll all be more comfortable than with that haughty French piece.' She became apologetic. 'Meaning no disrespect, Miss Rosamund, but I never dreamed the Master could be serious about a chit of a girl like you.'

The same thought was in Rosamund's mind as she went back into the sitting room to await Adrian's return, feeling suddenly shy.

He came at last and characteristically his first words were a reproof.

'You went to see Adela. You've been walking on that leg and I told you not to.'

'Oh, it's not that bad.'

He looked at her with a glint in his eyes. 'I'd better warn you, I shall refuse to let you omit "obey" from the marriage service.'

Rosamund laughed: 'Darling tyrant, your wishes are my law.'

He swooped upon her then, gathering her up in his arms, and seating her upon his knee.

'That's inaccurate,' he said, after he had kissed her. 'You'll always be able to twist me around your little finger.'

'That I doubt, but I daresay I'll manage to get round you when you become too despotic. Do I have to go on running?'

'Certainly not, unless you very much want to.'

She assured him she did not. 'Though it did bring us together,' she admitted. 'One thing about your reprehensible eavesdropping, we don't need to go into explanations. I expressed my feelings pretty plainly.'

'I wouldn't mind hearing you say it again,' he teased her.

'It's too late, I ought to be going home.'

'You could stay here.'

Feeling the urgency in his embrace and aware of her own rising excitement, she shook her head.

'I'd better go . . . safer.'

'Perhaps you're right.' He let her slip from his arms on to the sofa beside him. 'Do you approve of my recreation centre?'

'It's a wonderful idea. Are you going to coach any more runners?'

'Perhaps if I come across any local talent, but I'll stick to boys. Look where my one experiment with a girl has landed me!'

'If that's how you feel about it . . .' She tried to stand up.

'You'll learn how I feel when we're married,' he warned her and pulled her back on to his knees.

Later she said sadly:

'I never won that Olympic gold for you.'

'You won my heart, isn't that more worth having?'

'Infinitely, but it would be nice to have had both.'

'Never satisfied, are you, little glutton?'

'But are you?'

'Completely.'

'Then I am too,' she sighed, and surrendered to his kiss.

## Also available this month
## Four Titles in our Mills & Boon
## Classics Series

*Specially chosen re-issues of the best in
Romantic Fiction*

### May's Titles are:

### DARE I BE HAPPY?
*by Mary Burchell*

Marigold should have been blissfully happy in her marriage
to Paul Irving — but how could she, when the one man in the
world who could wreck it with a word was Paul's own
brother-in-law?

### THE CASTLE OF THE SEVEN LILACS
*by Violet Winspear*

When the handsome Baron Breck von Linden offered Siran
a job which involved staying at his fairytale home, the
Castle of the Seven Lilacs, she knew that it was attraction
for the Baron that was taking her there. But Breck's younger
brother Kurt made no secret of his opinion of Siran and
her motives. . . . .

### A MAN WITHOUT MERCY
*by Margery Hilton*

Compassion and loyalty — two endearing qualities, but they
had brought Gerda nothing but heartbreak. Compassion had
led her into a brief, tragic marriage. Now loyalty had forced
her into the power of the one man who could destroy her.
Because she loved Jordan Black as much as he despised her
— and he was a man without mercy . . . . .

### SOUTH TO FORGET
*by Essie Summers*

After an unhappy love affair Mary Rose wanted to get away
from everything, so when Ninian Macandrew, who had also
recently been jilted, asked her to go to his New Zealand
home with him as his fiancée it seemed the solution to her
problems. But "Oh what a tangled web we weave, when
first we practise to deceive"!

## Mills & Boon Classics
*— all that's great in Romantic Reading!*
**BUY THEM TODAY only 50p**

# Mills & Boon Present

## our first motion picture!
## Adapted from one of our most popular novels, Anne Mather's unforgettable "Leopard in the Snow."

### KEIR DULLEA · SUSAN PENHALIGON

*Leopard in the Snow*

Guest Stars
## KENNETH MORE · BILLIE WHITELAW

featuring GORDON THOMSON as MICHAEL
and JEREMY KEMP as BOLT

Produced by JOHN QUESTED and CHRIS HARROP
Screenplay by ANNE MATHER and JILL HYEM
Directed by GERRY O'HARA

An Anglo-Canadian Co-Production

## ON RELEASE DURING 1978
## IN UNITED KINGDOM, REP. OF IRELAND,
## AUSTRALIA AND NEW ZEALAND